DRAUPADI'S CHOICE

EXAMINING POLYANDRY IN HINDU MYTHOLOGY

SHAMPA CHATTERJEE

Dedication

For those who find wisdom in the complexities of ancient stories, and courage in the questions they continue to provoke.

Contents

Epigraph

"A woman is not a piece of property that she should be gifted away... She is an equal partner to man, his strength, and his support."
— Inspired by Draupadi's questioning in the Mahabharata

Foreword

When I first embarked on my journey as a Mindset and Relationship Coach, I never anticipated that one of my greatest teachers would be a character from an ancient epic. Yet Draupadi—fierce, complex, and extraordinarily resilient—has profoundly influenced both my personal understanding of relationships and my professional approach to helping others navigate their own.

As the founder of Mind Wave Hub, I have witnessed firsthand how deeply mythological archetypes continue to shape our modern understanding of ourselves and our relationships. The patterns established in these ancient narratives often unconsciously inform our expectations, behaviors, and emotional responses. This is why I believe examining these stories with fresh eyes is not merely an academic exercise but a practical tool for personal transformation.

Draupadi's polyandrous marriage to the five Pandava brothers has long been a subject of controversy and fascination. Some dismiss it as an anomaly, others try to explain it away through supernatural justification, and still others ignore it entirely as an inconvenient element of an otherwise inspirational story. But I have come to believe that it is precisely in these controversial aspects of our mythological heritage that the most profound wisdom often resides.

In this book, I have attempted to approach Draupadi's unusual marital arrangement not as a problem to be solved but as a multifaceted narrative that illuminates the complexity of human relationships, the tension between individual desire and social obligation, and the remarkable flexibility of Hindu tradition itself. By examining this single element of the Mahabharata through multiple lenses—historical, religious, feminist, and psychological—I hope to demonstrate how ancient stories continue to offer relevant insights for our contemporary struggles.

My work with clients has repeatedly shown me that when we engage honestly with complexity rather than seeking oversimplified answers, we create space for authentic growth and deeper understanding. It is my sincere hope that this exploration of Draupadi's extraordinary circumstances will inspire readers to approach both ancient wisdom and their own relationships with greater curiosity, compassion, and nuance.

The journey into understanding Draupadi's choice is, in many ways, a journey into understanding the countless choices we all make in our relationships—choices constrained by circumstance yet informed by our deepest values and aspirations. It is a journey I invite you to undertake with an open mind and heart.

Shampa Chatterjee
Mindset and Relationship Coach
Founder, Mind Wave Hub powered by Trustworthy Ties
April 2025

Preface

When I first encountered the story of Draupadi as a child, I was struck not by the grandeur of the Mahabharata's war or the philosophical depth of the Bhagavad Gita, but by a simple question: How could one woman be married to five brothers? This question, asked with childlike directness, touches upon one of the most enduring controversies within Hindu mythology—Draupadi's polyandrous marriage to the five Pandava brothers.

As I grew older and studied the epic in greater depth, I discovered that my childhood curiosity reflected centuries of scholarly debate, religious interpretation, and cultural negotiation. What seemed a simple narrative anomaly in fact opened windows into the complexities of gender relations, religious authority, historical context, and the evolution of Hindu tradition itself.

This slim volume does not attempt to provide definitive answers about Draupadi's unusual marriage. Rather, it seeks to explore the rich tapestry of interpretations that have emerged around this narrative element, from ancient commentaries to contemporary feminist readings. In doing so, it invites readers to consider how religious traditions accommodate controversial elements, how gender roles are negotiated through sacred narrative, and how ancient stories continue to generate meaning in contemporary life.

The study of mythology is not merely an archaeological excavation of past beliefs but an engagement with living traditions that continue to shape cultural consciousness. Draupadi's story, with all its complexities and contradictions, remains vibrantly alive in contemporary Hindu practice, artistic representation, and intellectual discourse. By examining the multiple interpretations of her polyandrous marriage, we gain insight not only into an ancient text but into the ongoing process by which communities make meaning from their sacred stories.

I offer this book as an invitation to thoughtful engagement with one of world literature's most fascinating female characters and the extraordinary circumstances of her life. Whether you approach this topic as a scholar, a practitioner, or simply a curious reader, my hope is that Draupadi's story will provoke the same sense of wonder and questioning that it first awakened in me many years ago.

Acknowledgements

This exploration of Draupadi's story would not have been possible without the contributions of numerous scholars whose work has shaped our understanding of this complex topic.

I am deeply indebted to Irawati Karve, whose pioneering work in "Yuganta: The End of an Epoch" offered one of the first feminist readings of Draupadi's character and marriage. Similarly, Chitra Banerjee Divakaruni's "The Palace of Illusions" revolutionized how we understand Draupadi's voice and perspective. Pratibha Ray's "Yajnaseni" provided invaluable insights into Draupadi's inner world and the complexities of her relationships.

For scholarly analysis of polyandry in Hindu contexts, I must acknowledge the foundational work of Wendy Doniger, whose extensive studies on gender and sexuality in Hindu mythology have been instrumental, particularly her insights in "The Hindus: An Alternative History" and "Women, Androgynes, and Other Mythical Beasts."

J.A.B. van Buitenen's definitive translation of the Mahabharata has been an indispensable resource, as has John Smith's work on marriage practices in ancient India. Alf Hiltebeitel's extensive scholarship on Draupadi worship in South India, particularly "The Cult of Draupadi," has been crucial for understanding her continuing religious significance.

My deepest appreciation goes to my family for their unwavering support throughout my life and every piece of my work.

Any errors or oversights in this book remain entirely my own.

Prologue

The great hall of Hastinapura falls silent. Five brothers sit frozen in shock as their mother's words hang in the air like suspended time: "Share what you have brought equally among yourselves." Kunti, matriarch of the Pandava family, has spoken without turning to see what her sons have "brought"—not realizing it is a woman, Draupadi, won by Arjuna at her svayamvara. A command once given cannot be withdrawn.

In this moment of stunned silence lies the seed of one of Hindu mythology's most enduring controversies.

Imagine Draupadi in this moment—a princess born of fire, raised to be a queen, now confronting a future unprecedented in royal lineages: marriage not to one prince, but to five brothers simultaneously. What thoughts crossed her mind? What choices, if any, were truly hers to make? The text offers us glimpses but leaves much to the imagination.

This singular moment—this apparent accident of fate—would shape not only Draupadi's destiny but generations of religious interpretation, social practice, and cultural understanding. A princess becoming wife to five brothers violates the very norms that the Mahabharata otherwise seems to uphold. Yet rather than being excised from the tradition, this narrative thread remains integral to the epic, demanding explanation, interpretation, and engagement from each generation that encounters it.

I first heard Draupadi's story as a child, sitting at my grandmother's feet during warm summer evenings. Like many Hindu children, I absorbed the Mahabharata not through formal study but through oral tradition—stories passed down, embellished, and made relevant through the skill of family storytellers. My grandmother spoke of Draupadi with particular reverence, emphasizing her strength, her devotion, and her endurance through extraordinary circumstances.

When I asked about her five husbands—a detail that naturally provoked a child's curiosity—my grandmother offered the traditional explanation of divine decree, karma from previous lives, and the necessity of family unity. Yet something in her voice suggested an awareness of deeper complexities beneath these explanations. Years later, I would come to understand that my grandmother, like countless storytellers before her, was navigating the delicate balance between preserving tradition and acknowledging its contradictions.

This book began from that childhood fascination and has evolved through years of formal study, conversations with scholars and practitioners, and reflection on the enduring power of controversial narratives. Why has Draupadi's polyandrous marriage remained so central to the Mahabharata tradition despite later Hindu orthodoxy's discomfort with the arrangement? What can this narrative element tell us about the flexibility of religious traditions more broadly? And how do contemporary readers—particularly women—find meaning in Draupadi's extraordinary circumstance?

As we explore these questions, I invite readers to approach this topic with both scholarly rigor and imaginative empathy. Draupadi stands at the intersection of divine purpose and human vulnerability, extraordinary circumstance and universal emotion. Her story resists simplistic interpretation precisely because it touches on fundamentally human questions about agency, duty, divine will, and the complex negotiation of personal desire within social constraint.

In many ways, Draupadi remains as she began—born of fire, defying categorization, challenging those who would reduce her to a simple lesson or moral exemplar. Her polyandrous marriage, rather than being a historical curiosity or theological anomaly, offers a window into how religious traditions accommodate contradiction, how sacred narratives generate ongoing meaning, and how ancient stories continue to illuminate contemporary questions.

The pages that follow offer not definitive answers but thoughtful exploration—an invitation to consider how this single narrative element reveals the dynamic, evolving nature of Hindu tradition and the enduring power of stories that trouble us, challenge us, and ultimately transform us.

Shampa Chatterjee

April 2025

Table Of Contents

- How major Hindu schools of thought have explained the marriage
- Dharmic justifications provided by commentators
- The concept of Draupadi as an incarnation of goddess Shri
- The tension between this story and later Hindu marriage laws

Chapter 4: Feminist and Modern Interpretations

- Contemporary feminist rereadings of Draupadi's agency
- Power dynamics within the polyandrous relationship
- Draupadi as a symbol of female strength and resilience
- Modern psychological and sociological analyses

Chapter 5: Cultural Impact and Contemporary Relevance

- How the story is portrayed in folk traditions, art, and performance
- Regional variations in how the polyandry is depicted
- Influence on modern literature and media
- How contemporary Hindu practitioners reconcile this story

Conclusion

- Synthesis of various perspectives
- The enduring relevance of Draupadi's story
- What this narrative reveals about the flexibility of Hindu tradition
- Final thoughts on how ancient controversial stories remain meaningful

Introduction

The Mahabharata: A Cornerstone of Hindu Civilization

The Mahabharata stands as one of humanity's most monumental literary achievements—a vast epic comprising over 100,000 verses that has shaped Hindu thought, spirituality, and social consciousness for millennia. More than merely a tale of the great Bharata dynasty and the cataclysmic Kurukshetra War, this ancient text serves as a repository of philosophical discourse, moral instruction, and theological revelation. The Bhagavad Gita, perhaps Hinduism's most influential scripture, emerges as a dialogue within this larger narrative tapestry. For countless generations across the Indian subcontinent and beyond, the Mahabharata has provided a framework through which people understand their relationship to divinity, society, and themselves.

What distinguishes the Mahabharata from many religious texts is its embrace of moral ambiguity. Unlike simpler narratives of good versus evil, the epic presents complex characters navigating ethically fraught situations where dharma (righteous duty) often appears contradictory or unclear. This complexity has allowed the text to remain vibrant and relevant across vastly different historical contexts. As the scholar A.K. Ramanujan famously noted, "No Hindu ever reads the Mahabharata for the first time"—its stories, characters, and dilemmas permeate cultural consciousness through oral traditions, ritual performances, visual arts, and modern media adaptations.

In contemporary Hindu society, the Mahabharata continues to function as both a sacred text and a living tradition that evolves through constant reinterpretation. Its characters serve as archetypes through which modern individuals understand themselves and their world. Among these figures, few have captured the imagination—or sparked as much controversy—as Draupadi, the woman whose extraordinary marriage stands at the center of this study.

Draupadi: Fire-Born Princess and Epic Heroine

Draupadi emerges from the Mahabharata not merely as a character but as a force of nature—literally born from sacrificial fire, an incarnation of the goddess Shri, destined to bring about the destruction of unrighteous warriors. Her very birth represents divine intervention in human affairs. As the daughter of King Drupada of Panchala, she enters the narrative already imbued with cosmic significance and extraordinary beauty.

Unlike many female characters in ancient epics who serve primarily as prizes or catalysts for male action, Draupadi possesses remarkable agency throughout the narrative. Her svayamvara (self-choice marriage ceremony) sets in motion central events of the epic. Her humiliation in the royal court—when the Kauravas attempt to disrobe her after she is staked and lost in a game of dice—becomes the spiritual and moral fulcrum of the entire story. Her vow not to bind her hair until it is washed in the blood of those who dishonored her stands as one of literature's most powerful expressions of righteous vengeance.

Throughout the epic, Draupadi embodies qualities rarely associated with female characters in ancient texts: fierce intelligence, unyielding determination, political acumen, and profound spiritual insight. She questions injustice even when it comes from divine sources. She holds her husbands accountable when they fail to live up to their responsibilities. In a narrative filled with male warriors, sages, and gods, Draupadi consistently emerges as one of the most dynamic and fully realized characters.

Yet despite—or perhaps because of—her centrality to the narrative, one aspect of Draupadi's life has remained perpetually controversial: her marriage to five men simultaneously.

The Polyandrous Marriage: A Challenge to Orthodox Frameworks

The circumstances of Draupadi's unusual marriage unfold when Arjuna, the third of the five Pandava brothers, wins her hand at her svayamvara by performing a nearly impossible feat of archery. Upon returning home with his prize, Arjuna's mother Kunti, without looking to see what her son has brought, instructs him to share it equally with his brothers—a command that, once uttered, cannot be rescinded according to the rules governing their family. Thus, through a mixture of fate, divine intervention, and familial obligation, Draupadi becomes wife to all five Pandava brothers: Yudhishthira, Bhima, Arjuna, Nakula, and Sahadeva.

This arrangement stands in stark contrast to the patriarchal, monogamous (for women) marriage system that would later become normative in Hindu society. While polygyny (a man having multiple wives) was common in ancient India, polyandry (a woman having multiple husbands) was rare and generally disapproved of in brahmanical texts. The epic itself acknowledges the extraordinary nature of this arrangement; multiple characters question its propriety, and elaborate justifications are provided within the narrative.

These justifications include:

1. A divine decree: The sage Vyasa explains that Draupadi is the incarnation of the goddess Shri, who had once prayed to Lord Shiva for a husband with five qualities. Shiva granted her wish literally, declaring she would have five husbands in her next life.
2. Karmic connection: In a previous life, Draupadi had performed such intense austerities that Shiva offered her a boon. She repeated her request for a husband five times, thus binding herself to five future husbands.
3. Practical necessity: The Pandavas are instructed to remain united for their safety and strength. Sharing Draupadi helps maintain their solidarity.

Despite these explanations, the polyandrous marriage remains one of the most contested elements of the epic. Conservative commentators throughout history have struggled to reconcile this arrangement with later Dharmashastra (law book) injunctions against polyandry. Some versions of the text minimize discussion of the practical aspects of this marriage, while others provide elaborate systems for how Draupadi divided her time among her husbands.

Thesis: The Continuing Challenge to Religious and Social Frameworks

Draupadi's polyandrous marriage stands as a profound challenge to simplistic understandings of Hindu tradition as monolithic or statically orthodox. This single narrative element—a woman with five husbands—continues to provoke debate, inspiration, and reinterpretation precisely because it defies easy categorization within conventional religious and social frameworks.

This study proposes that the enduring controversy surrounding Draupadi's marriage reveals several important truths about Hindu tradition:

First, it demonstrates that Hindu sacred texts contain elements that challenge later orthodox frameworks, suggesting a dynamic rather than static religious tradition. The presence of approved polyandry in one of Hinduism's most sacred texts indicates that marriage practices and gender roles have been more diverse and fluid throughout Hindu history than later normative texts might suggest.

Second, the various interpretations of Draupadi's marriage across different Hindu traditions reflect the religion's inherent pluralism. Rather than resolving this controversial element through dogmatic pronouncement, Hindu tradition has accommodated multiple, sometimes contradictory, readings of the same narrative.

Third, Draupadi's story continues to serve as a resource for contemporary challenges to patriarchal structures. Modern feminist readings of the Mahabharata often focus on Draupadi as a figure whose life contains both tremendous suffering under patriarchal constraints and remarkable resistance to those same constraints.

Finally, the persistence of this narrative in popular culture—across regional performances, literary retellings, television adaptations, and personal devotion—demonstrates how controversial elements often prove most culturally generative. Rather than being suppressed or forgotten, Draupadi's unusual marriage has become a focal point for ongoing cultural conversation about gender, power, divinity, and dharma.

As we move through more detailed analysis of the textual accounts, historical context, traditional interpretations, and contemporary readings of Draupadi's polyandrous marriage, this fundamental tension will remain our focus: how this single narrative element continues to challenge, inspire, and transform religious and social frameworks within the living tradition of Hinduism.

CHAPTER ONE

The Extraordinary Birth of the Fire-Born Princess

To understand the tangled threads of Draupadi's destiny—especially the question that still stirs wonder and discomfort in equal measure: *How did one woman come to marry five men?*—we must return to the moment she first emerged into the world. And that moment was anything but ordinary.

King Drupada of Panchala had fire in his heart and vengeance on his mind. Betrayed and humiliated by his childhood companion turned bitter rival, Drona, he turned to the sacred rites of fire sacrifice—not for peace, but for power. He sought a son, a warrior capable of restoring his pride and striking back against the insult carved into his memory.

But the fire gave him more than he asked for.

From the glowing heart of the yajna, two figures rose. First came Dhrishtadyumna, the son he had longed for. But then, as the flames danced higher, out stepped a dark-skinned girl—Krishnaa. Her skin shimmered like the night sky touched by fire, and her eyes carried the knowledge of lifetimes. She was not merely born. She arrived. With purpose. With prophecy.

The priest presiding over the ritual did not hesitate. "This dark-complexioned girl," he proclaimed, "will be the foremost of all women. Through her, the gods will accomplish their will. And because of her, chaos shall descend upon the Kshatriyas."

A strange blessing. A troubling omen.

From the very first breath she took, Draupadi was never just a daughter. She was a divine disruptor. Born not of the womb but of fire, she embodied heat, passion, danger, and the promise of transformation. She wasn't created to fit into the world. She was born to set it ablaze.

Her origin sets her apart from the very beginning—not merely as a princess, but as a cosmic force, a spark of the goddess Shri herself. It is as though her very nature was forged to challenge the order of things, to question the rules, to disrupt the comfort of tradition.

And perhaps, in that alone, lies the first clue as to why her marriage would never follow the path of convention.

The Svayamvara: A Contest for the Princess's Hand

Years passed, and the fire-born princess grew—into a woman whose beauty stirred hearts and whose presence unsettled even the proudest of kings. The time had come for her *svayamvara*—a sacred ritual where a woman could choose her husband from a gathering of worthy suitors. But this was not merely a gathering. This was a spectacle. A storm in waiting.

Kings and princes from all corners of the land assembled in the grand arena of Panchala. They came not just for her hand but to stake their pride, to tame the wild glory of a woman born from fire. Among them were Duryodhana, proud and ambitious, and Karna, the fierce and battle-hardened, both sons of the rival Kuru house.

But amidst the velvet of royalty and polished armor, five strangers watched quietly from the crowd—dressed as humble Brahmins, hiding from a world that had tried to burn them alive. These were the Pandavas: Yudhishthira, Bhima, Arjuna, Nakula, and Sahadeva, who had narrowly escaped a deadly trap set by their cousins, the Kauravas. Along with them was their mother, Kunti, cloaked in exile and survival.

The test that King Drupada had arranged was more than just difficult—it was near impossible. A mechanical fish spun high above a pool of still water. The task: string the great bow and pierce the fish's eye—not by looking at it directly, but only at its reflection shimmering in the water below.

One by one, the suitors tried—and failed. Arrogance shattered. Confidence bent. The arena, once full of certainty, began to hum with disbelief.

Then, from the edge of the gathering, stepped forward a man clad in the robes of a Brahmin—Arjuna, silent and calm, his fire masked by simplicity.

There were gasps. Protests. *"A Brahmin? Competing in a warrior's trial?"* But before the crowd could descend into outrage, Draupadi herself raised her voice—not loud, but clear enough to silence them all.

"The test is open to all," she said.

In that moment, Draupadi chose—not a man, but a possibility. She chose to see beyond caste, beyond expectation. Her voice cut through the tradition like a sword through silk.

And then, with grace that felt inevitable, Arjuna strung the bow and loosed the arrow.

The silence that followed was not mere shock—it was the breath the world takes when fate pivots. The arrow struck true. The eye of the fish shattered.

Victory.

The fire-born woman had found her match—not in title, but in spirit.

But the air shifted quickly. The princes and kings, their pride wounded, rose in protest. How could a man of no name, no throne, no lineage, dare win the princess of Panchala?

Yet Draupadi did not flinch. She had seen something they could not—valor beyond armor, divinity beneath disguise.

This was not just a contest. It was a quiet rebellion. It was the first time Draupadi chose for herself.

And though fate would soon twist her choice in ways she could never predict, in that arena, under the gaze of gods and men, she claimed her right to choose. And her fire burned brighter for it.

Kunti's Fateful Words: The Inadvertent Command

Triumphant, Arjuna returned from the *svayamvara*, his heart pounding not just with victory but with something deeper—recognition, perhaps, that he had just claimed more than a bride. He had won a spark of fate itself.

He and his brothers rushed back to the modest hut that had been their hidden refuge. Draupadi followed, not as a trophy, but as a flame silently crossing into shadows. Still dressed in her royal finery, she stepped into exile as though it were her birthright.

"Mother," Arjuna called from outside, his voice brimming with excitement, "See what we've brought today!"

Inside the hut, Kunti, weary and occupied, did not rise. She did not look. She simply replied, as mothers often do when life is lived in fragments and fatigue:

"Whatever it is, my sons, share it equally among yourselves."

The words fell softly, like ash from a fire long gone cold.

And then she stepped outside—and saw.

There, standing before her, was Draupadi. Regal. Vulnerable. Alive with divine presence. No fruit or alms, no weapon or garment. A woman. A princess. A future.

Kunti's face paled. Her breath caught.

In that moment, a simple sentence—uttered in innocence—tied fate into a knot no blade could cut. For a mother's word in that time, in that world, carried the weight of cosmic law. To retract it was to tempt chaos. To undo it was to betray dharma itself.

Her sons stood silent. So did Draupadi. The world held its breath.

Was this a mistake? Or was it design wearing the mask of accident?

The Mahabharata lets the ambiguity hang. And in that hanging, we are shown something essential about human fate: that it is not always chosen, nor always deserved. Sometimes, it arrives in the echo of someone else's voice.

The text preserves Kunti's dismay—yes, she regretted it. But she also feared the consequences of taking it back. **A promise, even unintended, once spoken, becomes sacred.** That is the weight dharma imposes.

And so, from a moment of motherly habit—spoken without sight or context—emerged the arrangement that would mark Draupadi's life forever.

Not by her word.

Not by her will.

But by the web of duty, expectation, and the heavy silence of those who feared doing wrong by doing what felt right.

And yet, the world would remember her not as a victim of this command, but as the woman who lived it with dignity, fire, and fierce devotion.

The Brothers' Dilemma: Debating the Marriage

The moment Kunti's words passed from echo to law, the five brothers stood before an invisible court—each held accountable not just to a mother, but to morality itself.

Yudhishthira, the eldest, bearer of justice, the one whose heart beat in rhythm with dharma, was the first to speak. His voice did not rise. It rarely did. But there was heaviness in it—a questioning that came not from fear, but from integrity.

"How can we, upholders of righteousness, commit what seems so unrighteous?"
"Can one woman belong to many men without dishonor?"

He was not accusing. He was pleading—for clarity, for righteousness to make itself known when the path was darkened by the weight of unintended consequence.

Beside him, Arjuna stirred. He, who had pierced the eye of the fish, who had heard Draupadi's silence and seen her soul across the crowd, now struggled with a different battle—**a claim he believed he had earned, but could not assert without tearing his family apart.**

Bhima, strong and loyal, looked not to the heavens, but to his mother. For him, her word was scripture. **"We cannot break her command,"** he said simply, with the unwavering clarity of a son who knew that obedience was also a kind of strength.

Nakula and Sahadeva, the youngest, said little. They watched, listened, absorbed. Sometimes, the hardest thing is to witness the people you revere be torn by righteousness itself.

The silence that wrapped around them was not empty. It was thick with questions no scripture could answer. The kind of questions that make even the most dharmic hearts tremble:

— Is obedience to one dharma a betrayal of another?

— Is a woman's fate negotiable, even when no wrong was intended?

— Can justice exist when no one is at fault, and yet someone must pay the price?

And then there was Draupadi.

Silent.

Absent from the debate about her own life.

She had chosen once—boldly, clearly—and now that choice was swept aside by a tangle of male duty, maternal word, and cosmic consequence. It is one of the great paradoxes of her story: a woman of immense strength, caught again and again in decisions made around her, about her, without her.

The text does not paint this moment with ease. It does not glorify it. Instead, it holds it up—raw, unresolved, sacred in its discomfort.

Because the Mahabharata, at its core, is not about easy answers. It is about the moments when all the answers feel wrong, and yet a choice must still be made.

And so, the brothers debated not as heroes, but as men—flawed, bound by love, law, and legacy.

And the world, once again, turned on the axis of a single woman's silence.

Divine Sanction and Precedent: Vyasa's Intervention

Just when the tension threatened to rupture the fragile bonds of duty and desire, he appeared—**Vyasa**, the sage who was not merely a witness to the Mahabharata but its soul, its author, its voice woven into the very bones of destiny.

The brothers, torn between obedience and righteousness, turned to him like weary pilgrims at the altar of wisdom.

And Vyasa, with eyes that had seen both past and future, spoke not just to them—but to the world.

He began, not with law, but with memory.

"Long ago," he said, **"in another life, this woman you now call Draupadi performed severe penance. Her soul—then unnamed—stood in devotion before Lord Shiva, seeking not just a husband, but perfection."**

She had asked for five qualities in a partner:

- *Virtue*
- *Strength*
- *Skill in arms*
- *Beauty*
- *Wisdom*

And Shiva, amused by the specificity, perhaps moved by her clarity, granted her prayer—not in one man, but five.

The five stood now before her—**each carrying one fragment of the ideal she had once begged the heavens**

for. Yudhishthira with his unshakable dharma. Bhima with his might. Arjuna with his warrior grace. Nakula, radiant in beauty. Sahadeva, quiet and wise.

This marriage was not a mistake. It was a fulfillment.

Vyasa revealed more. Draupadi was no ordinary woman; she was the earthly embodiment of **Shri**, the goddess of wealth, virtue, and cosmic balance. She had walked this earth to participate in a story far larger than herself—to ignite the war that would cleanse it of its rot.

He spoke of **Nalayani,** a woman from an ancient tale, faithful to her diseased husband, who had served him with such love and patience that she was granted a boon: **five husbands in her next life.** That woman's soul now lived in Draupadi.

He did not speak gently to avoid controversy. He spoke with the weight of celestial design.

And in his words, the impossible became ordained. The taboo became sacred. The discomfort became duty.

For in Vyasa's telling, **this was not about preference or accident—it was about necessity. About fate rippling backward and forward through time, aligning gods and mortals in a grand orchestration of karma.**

Even King Drupada, who had once dreamed of marrying his daughter to a single heroic son-in-law, bowed his head. He, too, was drawn into the web of this divine unfolding.

In the sage's voice, the marriage was no longer controversial.

It was inevitable.

And with that, the fire-born woman was to become the wife of five brothers—not by chance, nor by error, but by a promise the universe had made long before her first breath.

The Marriage Ceremony and Living Arrangements

With the sage's revelations echoing like sacred bells in the minds of all present, resistance dissolved like mist before morning light. King Drupada, though still reeling from the enormity of what was being asked of his daughter, yielded to the will of the divine. When Vyasa speaks, even kings set down their pride.

And so, in the sacred hush that follows revelation, the ceremonies began.

Draupadi, fire-born and fate-bound, married not one prince, but five.
One by one.
Brother after brother.
Each ritual performed with the proper Vedic rites, beginning with Yudhishthira—the eldest, the dharmic anchor of the Pandavas.

The text, curiously, offers little flourish here. It does not romanticize. It does not delve into embroidered details of bridal attire or festal joy. Instead, it offers something sparse, something... measured.

Perhaps because the narrative itself is walking a tightrope—**honoring a union that breaks every earthly norm.**

Yet within this solemnity is something deeply powerful: a woman standing at the heart of an arrangement so radical, so transgressive, that it shook the very roots of patriarchy—and yet was sanctified by gods, sages, and dharma itself.

Still, questions lingered—not of legitimacy, but of logistics.

And so, the brothers made an agreement. Simple, structured, sacred:

"Each year, Draupadi shall be the wife of one brother.
That year, her chamber shall be his alone.
If any other enters without need, he shall accept a twelve-year exile as penance."

It was law written not in stone, but in mutual honor.

This wasn't merely about preserving modesty—it was about **creating boundaries in a world where tradition had no map.** It was an effort to respect the woman they now all called wife, and to respect each other in turn.

Later tales whisper of how Draupadi, through divine grace or mystic power, would return to a state of purity each year—a virgin reborn for each husband. A story not about biology, but about the need to explain how such a thing could remain sacred in the eyes of a society so tightly wound with notions of purity and control.

And Draupadi?

The text tells us little about how she felt in these early days. But legends speak of her strength. Her discipline. Her ability to love equally, yet differently. To offer Bhima her soft laughter and Arjuna her silent eyes. To respect Yudhishthira's righteousness, nurture Sahadeva's wisdom, and admire Nakula's beauty—without dissolving herself in any of them.

She remained whole.

Not divided among five men.

But anchored in her own fire.

And so began the quiet, daily revolution of her life.

Challenges to the Arrangement: External Reactions

In the glow of ritual and divine blessing, the unusual marriage of Draupadi and the five Pandavas found its rhythm. But beyond the sacred chambers of Indraprastha, the world watched with raised eyebrows, tightened lips, and minds that could not stretch far enough to hold such a truth.

Not everyone was willing to see divinity in deviation.

Whispers followed her like shadows. Not from her husbands—who honored her with a devotion that bordered on reverence—but from others. Men who could not grasp what they could not control.

None more so than **Karna**.

Fierce, wounded, noble in pride but brutal in speech—Karna, again and again, referred to Draupadi as *"the shared wife,"* the woman of five husbands, as though that singular truth made her lesser.

And when her world crumbled during the infamous game of dice, when Yudhishthira gambled away not only his kingdom and his brothers but **her**, it was this polyandry that was dragged into the light like a crime.

In that cursed court, where dharma itself seemed to have fled, Draupadi stood alone, questioned for the legitimacy of her existence.

"How can you be lost in a wager?" they asked, *"A woman with five husbands—are you even bound to one?"*

Insults wrapped in mockery. Judgments flung like spears.

But Draupadi—burning with shame, fury, and unshakable grace—did not crumble. **She stood. She questioned.** She turned their words back on them with logic that cut sharper than any blade.

And still, the challenge remained—not just to her honor, but to the very arrangement of her life. As though her dignity depended not on her soul, but on the shape of her marriage.

What they did not see—what perhaps they *could not* see—was that Draupadi did not belong to five men. **She belonged to no one.**

She was wife, yes. But she was also queen. Strategist. Anchor. Firekeeper. The one whose voice they feared because it echoed truth in a chamber full of cowardice.

These external attacks were not just on her character. They were symptoms of a deeper disease—a world unequipped to honor female power that did not conform. A society that could celebrate multiple wives for men but recoiled at a woman who loved without singularity.

The Mahabharata does not hide these reactions. It does not erase the discomfort. Instead, it preserves them like relics—evidence of the world's limitations, and of the woman who survived them all.

Conclusion: The Textual Precedent and Its Implications

When a Marriage Becomes a Mirror for a Civilization

Draupadi's marriage to the five Pandavas is not a detail. It's not a subplot.
It is a fire that runs through the epic—warming some, burning others, and forever altering the landscape of dharma.

The Mahabharata does not explain it away with ease. It offers divine sanction, reincarnation logic, sage commentary, maternal missteps, and cosmic purpose—layer upon layer of justification.
Why?

Because even **then**, at the time of the epic's compilation—between 400 BCE and 400 CE—polyandry was controversial. Even in a world that allowed kings to have multiple wives, a woman with multiple husbands needed not just a reason, but a divine endorsement.

It's as though the storytellers themselves were aware of the **seismic shift** they were narrating. And yet, they did not censor it.

They enshrined it. **In one of the holiest texts of all time.**

And that tells us something.

It tells us that Draupadi's story was too powerful to erase, too rooted in cosmic design to disown.

This marriage—born of fire, anchored in dharma, and lived with fierce dignity—**became a paradox that Hindu tradition still wrestles with.**

Later *dharmaśāstra* texts, written by patriarchs with pens sharpened by orthodoxy, would outlaw polyandry. They would silence the messiness of divine contradiction. But Draupadi remained—untouched by their edits. A burning, brilliant reminder that the earliest spiritual narratives were far more expansive than we sometimes allow.

Her story stands at the threshold between worlds:

- Between law and love
- Between fate and free will
- Between womanhood as possession and womanhood as cosmic force

She was judged, tested, humiliated, yet never broken.
She was never "just" the wife of five men.
She was the woman the gods watched.

The one whose silence could shake an empire.
The one whose laughter could spark a war.
The one who held power not in her hands—but in her presence.

And as we move into the rest of her story—beyond the fires of birth and into the forests of betrayal, exile, and war—we carry this first chapter as a torch:

? A woman born not to fit the world—but to change it.

CHAPTER TWO

Polyandry in Ancient India: Beyond the Epic

When One Woman Was Enough for Many Men: Reframing the Forgotten Reality

Polyandry. Even the word stirs the mind with a kind of startled curiosity—perhaps because it challenges something ancient inside us. A script most of us didn't even know we inherited: that a woman belongs to one man, and that a man may, at times, belong to many women. But travel back—far back—into the earliest folds of Indian civilization, and that script begins to unravel. Quietly. Elegantly. Through the fire of a princess. Through the rhythm of Vedic verses. Through the lived lives of people long before laws were codified.

To understand Draupadi's marriage as anything more than divine exception or mythological spectacle, we must first unshackle ourselves from the lens of modern morality and post-Vedic orthodoxy. Because **polyandry in ancient India was not only possible—it was practiced.**

Not by the many, perhaps. But by the meaningful.

The Time Before Codification: A Fluid Landscape

Before laws like Manusmriti declared what a woman could or could not do, there was another India—one where dharma had not yet been captured in ink and where relationships were shaped not by rigid roles, but by real needs. That India, found in the folds of the Vedic age (roughly 1500 BCE to 500 BCE), reveals a world in motion. Not chaotic, but complex.

The **Rig Veda**, one of the oldest surviving texts in human history, whispers of a world that was deeply spiritual, deeply symbolic, and also socially experimental. Scholars and philologists have long debated a peculiar line in *Rig Veda 10.85.38*—a line that calls upon suitors to accept the bride being given to "one man." At first glance, it seems harmless. But to those reading between the ancient syllables, it suggests something more: **that the idea of multiple suitors or partners may have been familiar enough to require such clarification.** The need to say "to one man" is only needed when "to many" was also known.

If we take this seriously—and many scholars cautiously do—it means that **polyandrous dynamics may have been acknowledged, if not embraced, in Vedic societies.** Not necessarily as the norm, but as one of the possible rhythms of relational life.

The Mythical Echoes Within Vedic Lore

Myth, after all, is memory wrapped in metaphor. And in the Vedic world, metaphors held galaxies.

Take the story of **Saranyu**, the celestial wife of the sun god Vivasvan. In a lesser-known tale, she is said to have created a duplicate version of herself—a shadow being named Chhaya—to fulfill the role of wife when she herself could not. It is a tale rich in metaphor: one woman, two forms, fulfilling one role.

While this may not be literal polyandry, it opens the imaginative door to the idea of **shared wifehood**, multiplicity of roles, and the need for relational fluidity in the mythic consciousness of early Indian civilization.

Then there's **Gandhari**, mother of the Kauravas, whose vow to blindfold herself forever after marrying the blind king Dhritarashtra has often overshadowed another truth—**that she, too, exists in a narrative that questions the fixed nature of female roles**. In a world where women had agency, loyalty was not always synonymous with submission.

These women were not afterthoughts in a patriarchal world. They were forces of their own—complex, autonomous, divine, and very human.

Enter Draupadi: The Fire in the Fold

By the time the Mahabharata began to take shape—its early oral forms possibly composed around 800–400 BCE—the story of Draupadi may not have been radical. It may have been *remembered*. Preserved.

She, the fire-born woman, was not just a literary device or a symbol of divine wrath. She was **a vestige** of a time when polyandry was a practice woven into real social threads.

Her marriage to five brothers wasn't explained merely through divine boons and reincarnation logic to excuse a moral anomaly. No. It may have been a **cultural reflection** of a practice already known in certain tribal, pastoral, or mountainous communities. Her story, then, is not just exceptional—it is **representational**.

Dharmashastra and the Erasure of the Other Path

By the time **Manusmriti** and other Dharmashastra texts were compiled (circa 200 BCE – 200 CE), the tide had turned. Social conservatism was on the rise. Orthodoxy sought order. And with that came a clampdown on alternate ways of loving, living, and belonging.

Polyandry, being threatening to patriarchal inheritance models and spiritual hierarchies, was largely erased, deemed *adharmic*, and cast into the shadows of memory.

Yet Draupadi remained.

Unedited. Untouched.

Because she was not created by Brahmanical law. She was born of myth, memory, and maybe even **mountain winds and tribal fires**. She stood her ground as the wife of five. Not because she was permitted. But because she could not be erased.

Between Legend and Lived Reality

So, was polyandry common in Vedic India?

No. But neither was it *unimaginable*.

It existed on the margins, in the hills, in the wilds—among communities where **survival and solidarity shaped society more than scripture.**

Draupadi's story, then, may be understood as **a narrative echo of those spaces**, where a woman could belong to five men without shame, and where her role was not diminished but revered.

She is not an exception that proves the rule. She is the remnant of a rule that was written in an older tongue.

Social Structures and Economic Factors

Beyond Myth: What the Structure of Society Reveals About Its Stories

A story never lives in isolation.

It breathes the air of its time. It wears the garments of its culture. It carries the shape of the society that gave it voice.

So when we ask why Draupadi was allowed—no, **scripted**—to marry five men in the world of the Mahabharata, we must look not just at her character, but at the **world that made such a story make sense.**

That world was not a monolith. It was a **mosaic of tribal, pastoral, emerging urban**, and warrior communities. A transitional society—evolving from **kinship-based clans to organized kingdoms**, from oral lineages to codified law, from ritual freedom to spiritual standardization.

And in that **in-between** space, polyandry was more than plausible.

It was logical.

1. Fraternal Solidarity and Brotherhood Clans

One of the most striking features of the Mahabharata is its central family unit—the Pandavas. Five brothers, born of different divine fathers but raised together as one lineage. They **act as a unit**, fight as a unit, live as a unit—and, in Draupadi's case, marry as a unit.

This mirrors what anthropologists today would call a **"fraternal house-holding model"**—a structure in which **brothers cohabit and co-own** land, resources, and even, sometimes, wives.

Such arrangements preserve what is most sacred in early agrarian societies: **land, labor, and loyalty.**
Dividing a wife would be easier than dividing a kingdom.

In a tribal society where **the collective survival of the family outweighed individual rights**, the model of multiple brothers sharing one wife ensured:

- No inheritance fragmentation
- A united front in warfare
- Consolidated wealth
- And minimal familial conflict over property

It's no coincidence that **the Mahabharata's heroes embody this exact unity**, one that seems archaic through a modern lens but would have felt familiar—and perhaps even ideal—in certain ancient Indian tribal frameworks.

2. Economic Realities in Pastoral and Agrarian Societies

Let's talk pragmatism.

In subsistence farming communities or nomadic pastoralist groups, marriage was not just romance or ritual—it was **economic strategy**.

A single family with limited land could not afford to have five sons bringing five wives home—each demanding a share of inheritance and building separate households.

Fraternal polyandry **minimized economic pressure** on family resources. All sons stayed home. The wife, central to this arrangement, acted as:

- Manager of the household
- Equal partner in sustaining family lineage
- Emotional and practical anchor of a system rooted in **shared duty and trust**

Draupadi, with her rotation of one year per brother, perfectly exemplifies this model. One wife. Five partnerships. A system not of indulgence, but of **in-built discipline**.

This discipline wasn't mythical—it had social echoes. In real polyandrous societies, **timing, turn-taking, and personal boundaries** were upheld with seriousness. It wasn't just a custom—it was survival through structure.

3. Gender Roles: Less Patriarchal Than We Assume

Surprising as it may sound, **early Indian kinship societies**—especially in the pre-Dharmashastric era—weren't always rigidly patriarchal in the way later texts suggest.

In many tribal and matrilineal structures, women played powerful roles. Marriage wasn't just about transferring a woman from her natal home to her husband's—it was about forming **alliances**, ensuring **labor equilibrium**, and building **social harmony**.

Polyandry, especially in fraternal systems, actually **elevated the woman's role:**

- She was not disposable; she was central.
- She was not one among many wives; she was *the* wife.
- Her word, judgment, and emotional management often **held the family together.**

Draupadi embodies this. She is not cast as passive. She is sharp, spiritual, strategic.
She is the *keystone* of the Pandavas' house, not merely its ornament.

4. Legal Fluidity: Before Manusmriti's Grip

Before the rise of Brahmanical legalism, **regional customs** played a larger role in determining marriage norms.

India was, and is, a land of **coexisting legal systems**—what we today might call "customary law." This allowed for tremendous flexibility. A practice accepted in one region could be taboo in another. Marriage rules were negotiated by community needs, not national codes.

The **absence of condemnation** of Draupadi's marriage in early iterations of the Mahabharata hints that it was not immediately seen as scandalous. Later, as **Brahmanical orthodoxy grew** in influence, the story had to be *theologically justified*. But the original inclusion suggests societal openness—or at least **acquaintance—with the concept of polyandry.**

It wasn't outlawed.

It was narrated.

5. Warrior Brotherhoods and Political Alliances

Draupadi's marriage also reflects a **political logic**.

In tribal warrior bands, **strength came from solidarity.** Marrying one woman could become a **symbolic act of unity**, ensuring that no one brother's loyalty could be bought or fractured by separate marriage alliances.

A shared wife meant a **shared destiny**.

If the Pandavas had married five different princesses, their loyalties might have been split across five kingdoms. Draupadi **anchored them.** Spiritually. Strategically. Emotionally.

Social Structures Make Myth Plausible

Strip away the divine veil, and Draupadi's polyandrous marriage starts looking less like an epic exception and more like **a sophisticated echo of pre-urban kinship systems.** Her tale reflects a time when love, land, lineage, and loyalty were negotiated not by law books but by **the delicate balance of need and trust.**

What the Mahabharata records may be more than fiction.

It may be **a cultural memory**—a snapshot of a time before social norms hardened into law.

Archaeological and Ethnographic Evidence

Not Just in Story—But in Soil, Stone, and Shared Space

Legends can be questioned. Myths debated. But what happens when **the earth itself speaks?**

When we ask whether Draupadi's polyandrous marriage was merely symbolic or reflective of real practices, we must look not only at scripture or sociology, but at **the physical**

remnants of ancient lives: homes, burial grounds, social customs, and the **continued practices of people untouched by mainstream orthodoxy.**

Because while polyandry faded from formal law, it **never truly disappeared.**

It survived in the **slopes of the Himalayas,** in **village compounds,** and **in oral traditions passed from mother to daughter,** grandfather to grandson. The past has a habit of surviving where law forgets to look.

1. Echoes from Megasthenes: The Greek Eye on India

The earliest known Western account of polyandry in India comes from **Megasthenes,** a Greek ambassador at the court of Chandragupta Maurya in the 4th century BCE. Often treated with caution due to occasional exaggerations, his work *Indika* nonetheless offers intriguing observations.

He wrote of certain Indian communities where **"men of the same family shared one wife."**

This may seem anecdotal—but it is **startlingly aligned** with the precise arrangement of Draupadi's marriage. Even more significantly, Megasthenes wasn't describing the Mahabharata—he was recording what he *witnessed* or *was told about* firsthand.

Was this fraternal polyandry widespread? Unlikely. But it **was visible** enough to be documented by a foreign diplomat, centuries after the Mahabharata's formative oral composition had begun.

That matters.

It suggests that the **Mahabharata did not invent the concept**—it inherited, recorded, and sanctified it.

2. The Jataka Tales: Buddhist Stories of Social Reality

The **Jataka tales,** part of the Pali Canon of early Buddhism, offer another non-Brahmanical window into the ancient world. Compiled between the 4th century BCE and the 3rd century CE, these fables often incorporate real social practices, wrapped in moral teachings and rebirth narratives.

In stories like the **Kunala Jataka**, references to **polyandrous households** appear in **southern India** and **tribal communities**, with little judgment—just description.

The Jatakas are not epic poetry. They are **didactic mirrors** of everyday life.

If polyandry shows up there, it signals something crucial: **it was lived, and seen**, not just imagined or mythologized.

3. Harappan Remnants: Burials That Whisper Kinship

Moving further back in time, let us examine the **post-Harappan and late Harappan archaeological layers**—sites like **Kalibangan, Rakhigarhi, and Lothal.**

Here, we find household compounds large enough to **accommodate multiple adult males**, with **common courtyards and clustered burial patterns**. These setups are interpreted by some archaeologists as supporting **extended family living**, possibly with **non-monogamous or non-patriarchal relational structures**.

Do we find a skeleton labeled "polyandry"? Of course not.

But what we do find are **multiple male skeletons buried in the same residential spaces**, with **children's remains nearby**, suggesting **shared fatherhood, collective lineage**, or at the very least, **blurred lines of biological vs. social paternity**.

In other words, **polyandrous kinship structures are a plausible inference**—especially when we overlay these sites with oral traditions from communities in similar regions.

4. Living Fossils: Ethnographic Gold from the Himalayas

Where archaeology leaves gaps, anthropology fills them with lived experience. India's **Himalayan belt**—especially **Ladakh, Zanskar, Himachal Pradesh, and Uttarakhand**—is home to communities that practiced fraternal polyandry well into the **20th and even 21st century**.

Let's name a few:

• *Jaunsar-Bawar (Uttarakhand)*

In these highland communities, **brothers traditionally married a single woman**, who rotated between husbands based on a system of mutual respect and predetermined rules. Children belonged to the family, not any one man.

This mirrors Draupadi's arrangement almost exactly.

• *The Khasa People*

Among the Khasas (Western Himalayas), fraternal polyandry was structured with clear hierarchies: **the eldest brother had seniority**, and younger brothers respected the order of visitation and paternal identification.

In certain versions of the Mahabharata, **Yudhishthira is presented as Draupadi's primary husband**, reinforcing this resemblance.

• *The Toda Tribe (Nilgiri Hills, South India)*

The Todas practiced **polyandry with a ritual system**, including **a ceremonial fatherhood rite**, where the man who first touched a leaf to the pregnant woman's belly became the legal father—regardless of biological paternity.

Here again, the **emphasis was on collective parenting, shared responsibility, and social balance**, not monogamous ownership.

5. Memory in Practice: When Epic Shapes Life

What's truly fascinating is that many of these communities **justify their polyandry through reference to the Pandavas and Draupadi.**

"If she could do it, so can we," elders say.

This is not myth inspiring fiction.

It is **myth legitimizing memory—story as social license.**

In these places, the Mahabharata is not just a book. It is **ancestral law**—a cultural constitution that allows for variance, fluidity, and sacred exception.

6. Burial Sites and Shared Lineage in Himalayan Cultures

In communities where polyandry is practiced, burial rituals often reflect **non-linear descent**. In some Himalayan regions, **children are buried near maternal homes,** or under **collective paternal memorial stones,** rather than under single-family tombs.

These physical structures carry the imprints of **non-exclusive paternity,** echoing the Mahabharata's own reluctance to assign Draupadi's children to any one father definitively.

Material Culture Validates Mythical Structure

What does all this evidence tell us?

That **polyandry is not a mythological anomaly.**

It is a **pattern**—sometimes hidden, sometimes visible, often unacknowledged by dominant narratives.

The **Mahabharata, far from inventing it,** gave it voice. And the earth—from the stones of ancient Harappan homes to the hills of Uttarakhand—confirms that the voice was echoing something real.

Comparative Indo-European Mythological Patterns

Anomalous or Archetypal? Looking Beyond India's Borders

To some, Draupadi's polyandrous marriage is so singular, so strange, that it's often dismissed as either divine exception or narrative invention. But when we zoom out—across mythologies that share a common Indo-European ancestry—we begin to notice something quietly profound:

Polyandry may be rare, but the woman at its center is not.

Throughout Celtic, Norse, Greek, and other Indo-European mythologies, we find recurring figures—**sovereign women, boundary-crossers, untamed forces**—who, like Draupadi, disrupt the expected order of love, war, and power. They are not always polyandrous in a formal sense, but they bear emotional, symbolic, and sometimes sexual relationships with **multiple men**, and more importantly, with **multiple destinies**.

Let's meet them.

1. The Sovereignty Goddess in Celtic Myth: One Woman, Many Kings

In ancient **Irish and Celtic mythology**, there exists a recurring archetype: the **sovereignty goddess**. She is not just a consort or a deity of fertility—she **embodies the land itself**, and must be married or courted by the rightful king in order to **legitimize his rule**.

Here's the twist: **each king who rules must, in essence, "marry" her**, and she accepts multiple kings in succession—or in overlapping symbolism. Her relationships are not defined by monogamy or even emotional loyalty, but by **sacred power exchange**.

For instance, the goddess Ériu, from whom Ireland (Éire) takes its name, appears in various myth cycles as both lover and queen across multiple generations.

This mirrors Draupadi's role **as a symbol of cosmic dharma**, not just as a private woman but as a **spiritual tether anchoring multiple masculine energies** to a greater cause—**unity, justice, war, and transformation.**

2. Medb of Connacht: Sexual Autonomy in a Warrior Queen

Perhaps the most vivid example from Irish myth is **Queen Medb (Maeve)** of Connacht. She takes lovers freely, commands armies, and demands that her husbands be **without jealousy** and **equal in wealth and bravery**—or be replaced.

Her most famous epic, *The Táin Bó Cúailnge*, centers around her political and erotic dominance. While she doesn't formally marry multiple men at once, she wields **multi-partner power** in a way that **unsettles patriarchal norms.**

Like Draupadi, **her sexuality becomes a battlefield**, used against her, weaponized by enemies, and yet she survives as a symbol of unapologetic feminine force.

3. Freyja in Norse Myth: Goddess of Love and the Wild Will

In the poetic **Eddas of Norse mythology, Freyja** stands out as a goddess of love, war, and magic. Her beauty is renowned, and her romantic entanglements—both desired and despised by other gods—are numerous.

She is no one's possession.

She weeps tears of gold.

She rides into battle and chooses the slain.

She keeps secrets. She chooses her lovers. She leaves them when she must.

What binds Freyja to Draupadi is not marriage structure—but **symbolic autonomy**. Both are **central, irreplaceable, powerful,** and yet **constantly judged for the** very agency that makes them divine.

4. Helen of Troy: The Woman Who Sparked a War

In **Greek mythology**, **Helen of Troy** is the most immediate parallel to Draupadi in terms of epic function.

- She is **abducted—or elopes**, depending on the version.
- Her beauty is the subject of **desire, conflict, and moral chaos**.
- Her **marital status is contested**: wife to Menelaus, lover to Paris, a pawn in a geopolitical game, and yet she survives the war, returns, and **remains enshrined in legend**.

While Helen is not polyandrous in the narrative sense, her **multiple relational identities** destabilize the masculine order. Like Draupadi, she is used as an excuse for male rage, and yet her **voice is never silenced**, even when the world demands it.

5. Polyandry in the Shadows: Scythians and Tribal Practices

Let's turn to history's edge—where mythology bleeds into ethnography.

Greek historian **Herodotus** and others mention **tribal groups such as the Scythians**, among whom women had **more freedom**, including **forms of shared marital arrangements**. These were Indo-European nomadic warriors of the steppes—fierce, mobile, matriarchal in parts—and **their women rode horses, carried weapons, and chose their partners**.

Though the reports are often filtered through patriarchal Greek eyes (and must be read cautiously), they **hint at societies where polyandry—or at least relational plurality—was possible**.

Here, we find **cultural space for women like Draupadi**, who navigate shared husbands not through submission but through **ritual, rhythm, and power.**

6. Mythic Themes that Echo Draupadi Across Indo-European Worlds

Let's distill the patterns:

- **Sexual sovereignty**: Women choose or shift lovers, often for cosmic or political reasons.
- **Marital plurality**: While not always formalized as polyandry, women are connected to multiple men across time or narrative space.
- **War-bringing beauty**: Their bodies and choices are used by men to justify conflict.
- **Judged by patriarchy**: These women are glorified and vilified in equal measure—**either divine or dangerous, rarely both.**
- **Not mere lovers, but symbols**: Of land, fate, justice, and change.

This makes Draupadi part of a **global sisterhood of mythic disruption.**

7. Why Draupadi Remains Unique—And Why That Matters

And yet—**Draupadi is rare.**

Not just because of her polyandry, but because **her story was not erased.**

In most Indo-European traditions, women like her are **shoved to the margins**—their stories buried beneath conquest, empire, and religious reform.

But in India, **Draupadi survives.** She is worshipped in temples. Reimagined in literature. Cited in song. Studied in classrooms.

She is the only **epic, divine, mainstream heroine in Indo-European mythology** whose **polyandry is not just symbolic, but central—and sanctioned.**

Final Reflection: Not Alone—Just Unacknowledged

Draupadi's marriage was not just a literary anomaly. It was the **loudest voice among a chorus of silent sisters**—across mountains, myths, and civilizations.

By placing her story within a larger Indo-European context, we see how **female power, especially when entangled with sexuality, often challenges patriarchal norms—and is then explained away, suppressed, or mythologized beyond reach.**

But Draupadi is different.

She was not erased.

She was enshrined.

Not as a warning.

But as a fire that would not dim.

CHAPTER THREE

Reconciling the Extraordinary: Hindu Philosophical Schools on Draupadi's Marriage

A Sacred Dilemma: Five Husbands, One Soul

Among all the paradoxes in the Mahabharata—and there are many—none have stirred as much theological intrigue, curiosity, and quiet discomfort as the marriage of **one woman to five men.**

And not just any woman. **Draupadi.** The fire-born. The avenger. The queen. The wound and the witness.

Her polyandrous marriage is not a moral failure in the text. It is not punished. It is not undone. And yet, it doesn't quite fit into any **simple moral category.** So, what do you do with a woman whose very life bends the rules of dharma—but is still revered as dharmic?

You turn to the philosophers.

And in the vast, contemplative universe of Hindu philosophy, **they did not reject Draupadi.**
They **read her. Reframed her. Respected her.**

Sometimes as a symbol. Sometimes as a goddess. Always as something *beyond ordinary.*

Let's walk with them, school by school—through **Advaita, Dvaita, Vishishtadvaita, and Mimamsa**—and see how each opened new doors into Draupadi's extraordinary truth.

Advaita Vedanta: Beyond Duality, Beyond Convention

In the luminous halls of **Advaita Vedanta**, led by **Adi Shankaracharya**, the world is not divided but united. All form, all names, all dharma—they're just veils over the one supreme truth: **Brahman**.

So what, then, of a woman with five husbands?

To an Advaitin, this is not a question of morality, but of **metaphor**.

Not a scandal, but a **symbol**.

Draupadi, in this lens, is not just a woman. She becomes the **individual soul** (*jiva*)—pure consciousness, journeying through the **five senses**, the **five elements**, or the **five sheaths of being** (*koshas*). Her marriage is not about desire or duty—it's about experience. The soul, embodied, must interact with these five layers, learn from them, and finally rise beyond them.

Madhusudana Sarasvati, a powerful 16th-century Advaitic mystic, wrote that unusual stories in the epics are often not meant to instruct but to **illuminate**. Draupadi's marriage, in this view, isn't just permitted—it's **necessary**. A cosmic teaching. A flame that guides the reader past social conventions into the mystery of self-realization.

Because ultimately, in Advaita, there is no "other."

Draupadi is not the wife of five. She is **the self within all**.

Dvaita and Vishishtadvaita: When the Goddess Walks the Earth

In contrast, **Dvaita Vedanta**, founded by **Madhvacharya**, says the self and the divine are forever distinct. You are you. God is God. And devotion (*bhakti*) is the bridge.

Here, **Draupadi is not a symbol**. She is a **goddess. An avatar.**

In the Dvaita tradition, and its sibling, **Vishishtadvaita** (articulated by **Ramanuja**), Draupadi is seen as an incarnation of **Lakshmi**, the divine consort of Vishnu. She is **Shri**—the force of beauty, justice, abundance, and cosmic order.

Dvaita philosopher **Vyasatirtha**, writing in the 15th century, defends her marriage not by social logic, but by divine logic. Just as **Krishna's playful or rule-bending acts** are understood as part of his cosmic mission, Draupadi's marriage is seen as a **divine arrangement with a divine purpose.**

In Vishishtadvaita circles, Draupadi's five husbands are interpreted as **five forms or aspects of Vishnu**, and she—the feminine principle—is the unifying thread. Her presence among them is **not chaos, but coherence. Not anomaly, but archetype.**

Their marriage becomes **symbolic theology**—a sacred union of **diversity and devotion**, of **many forms and one essence.**

Mimamsa: The Ritual Thinkers and the Puzzle of Polyandry

And then we arrive at the **Mimamsakas**—keepers of precision, ritual, and textual clarity. For them, **dharma is action**, and scripture is law. So how did this meticulous tradition grapple with a woman married to five men?

With great care—and surprising flexibility.

Kumarila Bhatta, the 7th-century Mimamsa master, introduces the concept of **contextual dharma**—that rules change based on the **cosmic era (yuga)**. The Mahabharata is set in the **Dvapara Yuga**, a time when **dharma was more flexible, society more experimental**, and divine interventions more common. What was permitted then need not be applied now.

The Mimamsakas argue that **divine exceptions do not nullify general rules**. And since the Mahabharata itself offers divine reasoning—Shiva's boon, Draupadi's past-life austerities, and Vyasa's approval—the story **self-validates**.

Rather than throwing out the rulebook, Mimamsa simply says:

"This is not the rule. This is the exception."

A rare fire that burns outside the hearth of custom.

More Than Moral, More Than Myth

What's profound in all of these perspectives—non-dual, devotional, ritual—is the **intellectual generosity** with which they approach Draupadi. None of them reject her. None erase her. None declare her marriage immoral.

Instead, they ask deeper questions:

- *What is this marriage showing us?*
- *What does it symbolize about the soul, the goddess, or the era?*
- *Is this not a divine act wrapped in human clothing?*

And in doing so, they **preserve the paradox**—refusing to flatten it into doctrine, but elevating it into mystery.

A Living Tradition of Interpretation

Hindu philosophy, at its best, does not panic in the face of contradiction.

It contemplates. It expands. It rewrites the boundaries of understanding to include the **wild, the wondrous, and the seemingly impossible.**

Draupadi's marriage is one such wild flame. And the philosophers, each in their own way, let it burn—and **read its light instead of fearing its heat.**

Dharmic Justifications by Traditional Commentators

Scripture Doesn't Flinch—So Why Should We?

If we were to stand in that mythical courtroom where dharma itself is questioned—as Draupadi's marriage is placed on trial—we'd see that the first to rise in her defense isn't a priest or a king.

It's **Vyasa**. The sage. The seer. The storyteller who wrote the very world she lived in.

And from that moment onward, a lineage of traditional commentators—philosophers, jurists, poets, and saints—picked up the mantle. Not to *excuse* her marriage. But to **uphold it**.

To say: **This was no accident. This was no sin. This was sacred.**

Vyasa's Voice: The First Witness

Vyasa's explanations, woven directly into the Mahabharata, are far more than narrative devices. They are **divine testimony**.

When Draupadi's marriage is questioned, **Vyasa offers three truths**—each one like a jewel in the flame:

1. **The Past-Life Vow**: He reveals that Draupadi, in a previous birth, was the daughter of a sage. She performed severe austerities and begged Lord Shiva for a husband possessing **five distinct virtues**—strength, wisdom, beauty, skill, and righteousness. She asked not once, but five times. Shiva, smiling, granted her wish literally. In her next birth, she would marry **five men**, each embodying one of those virtues.

2. **The Goddess in Disguise**: Vyasa identifies her as the incarnation of **Shri (Lakshmi)**—the divine feminine, born not from a womb but from fire, here to participate in the restoration of cosmic balance.
3. **The Indra Connection**: He reveals the Pandavas as **partial incarnations of Indra**, and Draupadi as the shared consort they are destined to honor. In this telling, her polyandry isn't deviation—it's **divine design**.

These are not casual justifications. They are foundational truths for traditional commentators who would come centuries later. Vyasa's voice becomes a **seal of cosmic authority**, a source no sage dares contradict.

Kunti's Command: When a Mother's Word Becomes Law

Another line of justification comes not from the heavens, but from the hearth.

It begins with **Kunti's fateful instruction**—"Whatever you have brought, share it equally." A mother's command, spoken in innocence, that suddenly becomes dharma.

The 14th-century commentator **Devabodha** writes that **a mother's word carries the sanctity of divine law**—especially in families bound by truth. For the Pandavas to disobey Kunti, even unintentionally, would be a **graver dharmic violation** than breaking social custom.

And so, **matriarchal authority becomes the moral anchor.** The fire-born queen is shared, not out of lust or confusion, but out of **loyalty to dharma as spoken by a mother's tongue.**

Later, **Arjunamisha** (15th century) affirms this hierarchy of duties. He states plainly:

"When marriage law conflicts with maternal command, the latter prevails—for the parent is the first teacher of dharma."

This interpretation is not about hierarchy for its own sake. It's about the emotional and spiritual **integrity of obedience, intention, and family honor**—all of which Draupadi's marriage preserves, not disrupts.

Shiva's Blessing: When the Divine Himself Nods

In some versions of the Mahabharata, the Pandavas, before fully accepting the shared marriage, **seek Lord Shiva's blessing**.

And he gives it.

The 16th-century commentator **Kataka Lokanatha** writes that this moment is crucial. **Divine sanction** is not symbolic. It is dharma-altering. If Shiva blesses an arrangement, no priest or philosopher may oppose it.

Just as Krishna's acts in the Bhagavad Gita transcend human law to serve higher purpose, **so too does Shiva's nod elevate the marriage from exception to exaltation.**

In this telling, Draupadi's role becomes almost priestly—**an embodied yajna**, where divine will is enacted through her body, her consent, her dignity.

The Authority of the Author

The 12th-century scholar **Nilakantha Chaturdhara**, in his revered Mahabharata commentary, makes a striking point:

"Vyasa's word must be accepted as final—not only because he is the narrator, but because he is a rishi of divine insight."

To reject Vyasa's explanation would be to **undermine the narrative itself.** And so, Draupadi's marriage becomes **canonically dharmic**—not despite its strangeness, but because it is *explained within the sacred text.*

In a tradition where scriptural integrity is paramount, **in-text justification becomes theological validation.**

Draupadi Is Not Ashamed—So Why Are We?

Across these commentaries, one thread remains consistent:

Draupadi is never punished. Never silenced. Never shamed. Her marriage is questioned, yes. But **she is never declared impure.**

This is important.

Because in Hindu tradition, **purity is spiritual, not sexual.** It is about intention, duty, and divine alignment.

And by these standards, **Draupadi shines**.

Her loyalty to each husband, her poise, her silence in moments of chaos, her fierce voice in moments of injustice—**they become the real dharma.**

The traditional commentators do not squirm.

They do not explain her away.

They do not erase her.

They **lift her**—into the domain of **goddesses and vows, fire and fate.**

Draupadi as Goddess Incarnate: Theological Implications

Born of Fire, Not Flesh

The Mahabharata does not begin Draupadi's story with a cradle. It begins with a **sacrificial fire**. She emerges not from a womb, but from flames—already grown, already destined, already watched by gods.

Her origin is not just unusual—it is **symbolic. Ritual. Sacred.**

She is **ayonija**—not born of the womb. And in Hindu cosmology, such a birth isn't a lack of motherhood—it's a sign of divine purpose. Whenever cosmic balance is threatened, **the divine feminine descends**, not gently, but like lightning. Or fire.

And fire, as we know, does not compromise.

Shri on Earth: The Evolution of a Divine Identity

Though the Mahabharata does not initially name Draupadi as **Shri or Lakshmi**, later traditions, regional tellings, and theological commentaries begin to pull her into **divine orbit.**

Over time, she is not just treated as divine—she is declared as such:

- In **Southern recensions** of the Mahabharata, her divine identity is emphasized more clearly than in the Northern versions.
- By the **13th century**, Madhvacharya (Anandatirtha) proclaims her to be **Bharati Devi**, a form of Lakshmi.
- In various **Vaishnava traditions**, she is understood as **Shri**—the goddess of fortune, abundance, and grace—married simultaneously to multiple aspects of Vishnu.

Her five husbands, then, are not just men. They are **the five expressions of the divine masculine.** And she is the one who binds them—not with lust or law, but with **cosmic necessity.**

Why Her Divinity Matters

To understand the depth of this interpretation, we must remember a central truth in Hindu theology:

The divine does not always follow the rules of the world.It rewrites them.

If Draupadi is an incarnation of Shri, then her choices—and even the strangeness of her marriage—cannot be judged by human standards.

The 17th-century commentator **Nilakantha** says it plainly:

"Divine incarnations act not for personal gain, but to serve a greater cosmic plan. Their dharma transcends ours."

So, when Draupadi becomes the shared wife of the Pandavas, it is not about sexuality or deviation.

It is about **holding the world together.** About ensuring that five men, five egos, five destinies—**remain bound by one fire.**

Transcending Dharma, Not Violating It

In traditional Hindu thought, the divine often breaks rules to reveal **higher order:**

- Krishna lies, cheats, and even dances on the battlefield—but only to restore dharma.
- Shiva wears ashes and lives in cremation grounds—yet is called *Mahadeva*, the Great God.
- Sita walks into fire not to prove herself—but to return to her cosmic form.

Likewise, Draupadi, **as goddess**, becomes the **pivot** upon which the wheel of destiny turns. Her polyandry is **not a scandal to be explained away**, but **a spiritual tool** to serve cosmic purpose.

The **Vaishnava thinker Vallabhacharya** saw her marriage as a **metaphor for unity in multiplicity.** The one (Draupadi) belongs to many (the Pandavas), just as the one soul connects to many expressions of the divine.

The Dance of Divine Feminine and Masculine

In many **symbolic interpretations**, Draupadi's relationship with her five husbands represents the **dance between the feminine principle (Shakti)** and the **varied** expressions of the masculine divine (Vishnu's forms).

Each husband embodies a **different spiritual quality**:

- **Yudhishthira**: Dharma (Justice)
- **Bhima**: Bala (Strength)
- **Arjuna**: Jnana (Knowledge)
- **Nakula**: Saundarya (Beauty)
- **Sahadeva**: Buddhi (Wisdom)

And Draupadi? She is the **Shri** that **binds them, complements them**, and **guides them**.

This theological lens transforms her marriage from a domestic arrangement into **a cosmic model of harmony**.

The Regional Goddess: Draupadi Amman in South India

And perhaps the most living, breathing proof of her divinity lies **not in texts, but in temples**.

In **Tamil Nadu**, Draupadi is not just remembered—**she is worshipped**.

She becomes **Draupadi Amman**, a **guardian goddess**, the **flame of justice**, and the **protector of the people**. In village shrines, she is depicted with open arms or a sword in hand—**goddess of both compassion and wrath**.

The folk traditions do not intellectualize her polyandry. They celebrate her as:

- The woman who stood against shame.
- The one who demanded justice in a court of silence.
- The queen who became a goddess to avenge wrongs and restore balance.

Her marriage, in this worldview, is not an issue—it is an **expansion** of her divine heart. She belongs to five because she has the **capacity to love, protect, and contain more than one soul.**

Symbolic Readings: A Divine Mirror for Us All

Traditional thinkers like **Vedantadesika** suggest that Draupadi's divine birth, pain, and unusual path serve **as a mirror**—not just for her husbands, but for **all of us.**

She exposes the weaknesses in others.

She evokes their courage. She tests their vows. She triggers transformation.

That's what goddesses do.

They don't just bless. They **burn away illusion.**

The Divine Feminine Does Not Need to Apologize

Perhaps the most important theological implication of Draupadi's divine identity is this:

She does not need to be explained away.

She needs to be **honored.**

Her choices, her pain, her fire—they are not problems. They are **part of the design**. And the tradition, to its credit, has found space to **venerate her not despite her marriage, but because of it.**

She is **Lakshmi in fire,**

Justice in woman's form,

A queen among gods,

A goddess among men.

Tensions with Later Hindu Marriage Laws

The Lawbooks Whisper: "She Is the Exception"

*For centuries, storytellers and spiritual seers lifted Draupadi up—honoring her marriage, her fire, her divine birth. But as the centuries turned, and **India's dharmic tradition grew*** *more codified, something began to shift.*

Laws were written. Norms were defined. Order became preservation.

And in this tightening web of **legal and social control**, polyandry—especially for women—was quietly but firmly outlawed.

Not with rage. Not with punishment. But with something perhaps more powerful: **erasure by omission**.

Dharmashastras and the Rise of Monogamous Idealism

Texts like **Manusmriti, Parashara Smriti**, and the later **nibandha digests** (legal commentaries like *Mitakshara* and *Nirnayasindhu*) laid down strict prescriptions about marriage.

And one thing they agreed on:

A woman may not have more than one husband.

This was now **Stridharma**—the law of a woman's duty. Her loyalty, her sexual exclusivity, and her role in maintaining family honor were **no longer flexible or contextual**—they were **absolute**.

In the **Kali Yuga**, the current age of decline and chaos, women were expected to be the keepers of purity—often at the cost of their freedom.

Polyandry, in this legal system, was **not only taboo—it was forbidden.**

So What About Draupadi?

How did the tradition reconcile this contradiction? How could it continue to **worship** a woman whose life blatantly defied the rules it now demanded?

It didn't erase her.

Instead, it did something more nuanced—**it named her an exception.**

Over and over again, legal thinkers, theologians, and jurists said:

"Yes, she did it. But she's not like us. She's not human. She's not here. She was allowed because the universe needed it."

This is what makes Hindu legal thinking unique: **it separates the mythic from the mundane, the sacred from the replicable.**

Yuga Dharma: The Law of Ages

Perhaps the most elegant solution came through the **doctrine of yugas**—the four cosmic ages that govern human conduct and morality:

1. **Satya Yuga** – Age of Truth
2. **Treta Yuga** – Age of Ritual
3. **Dvapara Yuga** – Age of Heroism (where Mahabharata is set)
4. **Kali Yuga** – Age of Conflict (our present)

Legal scholars, like the 16th-century jurist **Kamalakara Bhatta,** used this framework to resolve the tension:

"What was permitted in Dvapara Yuga is not permitted in Kali Yuga."

It's a simple yet powerful logic:

Draupadi's marriage was allowed then—not now.

The divine timeline becomes a **moral firewall.** It shields the story from imitation while preserving its sanctity.

The Exception That Proves the Rule

The phrase echoed through commentaries:

"Draupadi is not the rule. She is the exception."

Balambhatta, a 17th-century thinker, said it clearly:

"Her case *proves* the rule, by breaking it so completely—and yet being divinely sanctioned."

In other words, Draupadi's story becomes a **controlled fire**—not to be extinguished, but not to be reproduced either.

And this tension is not treated as a threat to the tradition. It's treated as its **beauty.**

Why No Legal Precedents Emerged

Despite her story's central place in Hindu memory, no **traditional Hindu legal ruling**—no royal edict, no village code, no priestly instruction—**ever used Draupadi's marriage as precedent** to allow polyandry for women.

Not once.

Even in regions where **tribal and customary polyandry was practiced** (like the Himalayas), the justification was cultural—not scriptural.

This silence is telling. It shows a quiet agreement between **spiritual reverence and legal distance.**

The **Mahabharata was kept sacred.** But it was not **legal code.**

The Woman Between Two Worlds

And what of Draupadi, in this legal landscape?

She stands, once again, **between acceptance and restriction, divinity and danger.**

She is honored, not copied. Revered, not repeated.

She is remembered in temples and in texts. But no daughter is raised to follow her path.

It is both beautiful and tragic.

She becomes **a sacred wound in the heart of dharma**—a reminder that sometimes, the rules must bend so that justice can rise.

A Tradition That Refuses to Flatten

What emerges from this legal-theological dance is not hypocrisy, but a kind of **Hindu hermeneutic resilience.**

The tradition does not reject contradiction. It **narrates through it.**

It builds layered responses:

- "She was divine."
- "It was a different age."
- "It was a cosmic purpose."
- "It was a mother's command."
- "It was Vyasa's will."

Each response **softens the rupture,** until **the anomaly becomes sacred.**

And Yet, She Stays

Despite all prohibitions, **Draupadi remains untouched.**

She is not rewritten to fit later laws.

She is not shamed into silence.

She is not erased from the canon.

She remains—**the only woman in all of Hindu scripture who marries five men and is still called chaste, divine, and dharmic.**

And that, perhaps, is the tradition's greatest act of courage.

Conclusion: The Theological Productivity of Controversy

What Do You Do With a Woman Who Breaks Every Rule—But Still Feels Holy?

You listen.

You wrestle.

You remember.

And eventually...

You make her sacred.

This is what Hindu tradition did with Draupadi.

Not by pretending her marriage was ordinary.

Not by trying to rewrite the rules she broke.

But by doing something far more radical:

Making room for the contradiction.

A Tradition that Dances with Complexity

In many religious traditions, controversy leads to exclusion. The moment something doesn't fit the moral mold, it is cast out, disowned, or silenced. But **Hinduism does something else**. Something more ancient. More courageous.

It turns controversy into contemplation.

It invites contradiction into the circle and says:

"What are you here to teach us?"

Draupadi's polyandrous marriage became **theological fuel**—sparking centuries of reflection across schools, texts, and temples.

- **Advaitins** turned her into a symbol of the soul entangled in the five senses.
- **Dvaitins and Vishishtadvaitins** lifted her into the sky as Lakshmi herself, choosing not one god, but five forms of him.
- **Mimamsakas** accepted her and moved on—because the fire of dharma shifts with the age.
- **Legal jurists** respected her, but contained her.
- **Poets worshipped her.**
- **Villagers built temples to her.**

And in all of it, no one dared to say she was wrong.

Because **how could the divine be wrong?**

Her Story Is Not a Footnote. It Is a Flame.

Draupadi's marriage is not just an epic event. It is a reminder that **truth cannot always be clean**, and **divinity does not always arrive wearing the robes we expect.**

She challenges not only laws, but the very **idea of what it means to be pure, powerful, and dharmic.**

She is not contained by her pain.
She is not humbled by her humiliation.
She is not erased by her exceptionality.

She is the fire that survived five husbands, one war, and a thousand judgments.

The Sacred Function of Her Controversy

If her story had been easy, we would not still be talking about her.

It is the **difficulty** of her life that makes her spiritually fertile ground.

Her marriage raised difficult questions—
But those questions made the tradition **smarter. Softer. Braver.**

Every commentator who tried to explain her, justify her, sanctify her—was **deepening Hindu thought**, stretching its categories, daring it to hold more.

This is the **productive power of theological discomfort.** It doesn't destroy faith. It **forces it to evolve.**

Not a Blueprint—But a Mirror

No one was meant to imitate Draupadi.
But everyone was meant to **reflect** in her.

Her life is not a manual. It is a **mirror**—showing us:

- What we do with women who don't fit the mold
- How we make space for power wrapped in paradox
- And how our greatest scriptures are not scared of the untidy

She is not a goddess because she was perfect.

She is a goddess because she **was not afraid to be complex**.

This Is the Hindu Way: Never Throw Away the Flame

In the end, Draupadi's story reveals the soul of the tradition that birthed her:

A tradition that holds paradox like prayer beads. That lets fire burn through its laws, and still calls it sacred. That believes the **unusual, the painful, the powerful**—are not deviations, but **invitations to look deeper**.

So when we see Draupadi, we do not just see five husbands.

We see five truths. Five mirrors. Five possibilities.

And we see a woman who could not be confined by rules—

So the tradition wrapped her in **myth, fire, philosophy, and reverence** instead.

Not because she broke dharma.

But because she **expanded it**.

CHAPTER FOUR

Contemporary Feminist Rereadings of Draupadi's Agency

God, I love how much our understanding of Draupadi has changed over the last 50 years. Before the 1970s, she was basically stuck in these two boring boxes: either she was the troublemaker who caused a catastrophic war, or she was this impossibly patient wife who somehow managed to be devoted to five husbands at once. Talk about a false choice!

Then feminist scholars came along and blew up the whole framework. They started asking the questions nobody had bothered with before. Did Draupadi actually have any say in her marriages? When did she push back against the men controlling her life? How did she carve out agency in a world designed to deny it to her?

Irawati Karve's *Yuganta* (1969) was the first real breakthrough. Instead of seeing Draupadi as this passive figure just accepting whatever weird arrangement the men in her life created, Karve showed her as someone actively navigating really complicated power structures. Remember how furious Draupadi gets after the dice game when her husbands fail to protect her? Traditional commentators would call her shrill or unreasonable. Karve said, no - that's legitimate moral and political critique. She's calling out the entire patriarchal system.

Ruth Vanita took this idea and ran with it. She zeroed in on those moments where Draupadi clearly exercises agency despite everything stacked against her. Like that incredible moment during the dice game when she asks, "If Yudhishthira had already lost himself, how could he stake me?" That's not just a woman being clever - that's someone challenging the entire legal and philosophical framework of the assembly. Or when everyone pressures her to forgive her abusers, and she straight-up refuses. In traditional interpretations, she's stubborn. In feminist readings, she's demanding accountability.

I'm particularly fascinated by what Mahasweta Devi did with her short story "Draupadi" (1981). She completely reimagined the character in the context of the Naxalite rebellion in West Bengal. Her protagonist is a tribal woman named Dopdi (which is just a regional pronunciation of Draupadi), creating this powerful link between mythic resistance and contemporary struggles against state violence. After Dopdi is captured and gang-raped by police officers, she refuses to cover her body - instead, she uses her nakedness as a weapon against her abusers. It's a direct callback to the attempted disrobing in the Mahabharata, but with a shocking modern twist.

The polyandrous marriage itself has become a major focus for feminist scholars. It's wild how traditional versions of the story barely mention whether Draupadi consented to marry five men. As Stephanie Jamison and Lindsey Harlan point out, the arrangement was decided between the Pandavas and their mother, Kunti - nobody actually asked Draupadi how she felt about it. Which is why many feminist readings see this marriage not as some divine blessing or spiritual opportunity (which is how traditional commentaries frame it) but as the first in a series of violations that Draupadi experiences throughout the epic.

That said, not all feminist scholars treat Draupadi as simply a victim. Alf Hiltebeitel and Vrinda Nabar suggest that within the constraints of her society, Draupadi strategically leveraged her unusual position to secure forms of power and influence that other women couldn't access. Her relationships with each husband gave her different types of authority - from Yudhishthira's political power to Bhima's unwavering loyalty. In this reading, Draupadi isn't just passively accepting a weird marital arrangement; she's transforming it into a source of social capital.

You can see this complex approach in Pratibha Ray's novel *Yajnaseni* (1984). Told from Draupadi's perspective, it portrays her polyandrous marriage as initially unwanted but eventually transformed into something that enables her personal and spiritual growth. Ray's Draupadi moves from confusion and resentment to a deeper understanding of her role, though she never stops calling out injustice when she sees it.

Power Dynamics Within the Polyandrous Relationship

Modern scholars have been obsessed with unpacking the power dynamics between Draupadi and her five husbands - something traditional accounts tend to gloss over with vague spiritual justifications. The epic itself gives us some structure: the brothers had a rotating schedule, with each husband getting exclusive access to Draupadi for a year at a time. If any brother interrupted another's time with her, he had to go on a year-long pilgrimage and practice celibacy - a rule that Arjuna actually breaks when he barges into Yudhishthira's chamber to grab some weapons during a cattle raid.

But contemporary analyses dig way deeper than these logistics. They look at the emotional, sexual, and political dimensions of this bizarre arrangement. Several key patterns emerge:

First, the relationships were clearly unequal. The epic hints that Arjuna was Draupadi's favorite - after all, she had originally expected to marry only him after he won that archery contest at her svayamvara. Depending on which regional version you read, she had a particular attachment to either Arjuna or Bhima, with Bhima often portrayed as her most devoted protector and the only husband who consistently puts her welfare above all other considerations.

Second, Draupadi's relationships with each husband reflect different aspects of power and vulnerability. With Yudhishthira, the eldest brother and king, her relationship highlights all these tensions between royal duty and personal loyalty - which explodes when he stakes her in that dice game. With Bhima, the strongest but often marginalized brother, she forms this alliance based on their shared experiences of being disrespected within the family. With Arjuna, considered the most skilled and favored brother, her relationship gets complicated by polygamy issues, since she has to share him with other wives, including Krishna's sister Subhadra.

Sudhir Kakar took a psychoanalytic approach in *The Inner World* (1978), suggesting that the polyandrous arrangement reflects broader Indian cultural patterns around mother-son relationships. In his reading, Draupadi serves as this shared maternal figure who preserves the brothers' bonds while channeling competitive impulses away from direct confrontation. Gayatri Spivak absolutely hated this interpretation, arguing that it reduces Draupadi to a psychological function instead of recognizing her as a person with her own desires and agency.

More recent sociological analyses have applied modern relationship concepts. Veena Das examines how the arrangement creates what we'd now call a "polycule" - a network of interconnected relationships that go beyond simple one-on-one bonds. Draupadi isn't just a wife to five individuals but the central node in this complex relational network that includes her husbands' relationships with each other, with their other wives, and with extended family members.

These analyses reveal that far from being just "five men sharing one woman" (which is how it's often simplistically described), the polyandrous marriage creates this intricate social ecosystem that both reflects and reconfigures traditional patriarchal structures. Draupadi has to navigate not just her relationships with individual husbands but this entire network of power, loyalty, and obligation surrounding them. What's remarkable is her ability to maintain her voice and agency within this crazy-complex system.

Draupadi as a Symbol of Female Strength and Resilience

Beyond academic analysis, Draupadi has become this powerful symbol of female strength and resilience in contemporary culture. She's transformed from being a marginal figure in traditional religious commentary to a central icon in feminist Hindu thought, reflecting broader shifts in how we understand gender, power, and spirituality.

That pivotal moment - her attempted disrobing in the Kaurava court - has been completely reclaimed in modern interpretations. Traditional accounts focus on Krishna's divine intervention, with the god miraculously extending Draupadi's sari to prevent her humiliation. While that's still spiritually significant, contemporary readings have shifted attention to what Draupadi does before the miracle: her questioning of the legal and moral basis for her treatment, her calling out of the elders who remain silent in the face of injustice, and her prophetic declaration that this dishonor will ultimately destroy the entire Kuru lineage.

In modern Indian feminist discourse, "being Draupadi" has become shorthand for women's resistance to patriarchal violence. The playwright Mahashweta Bhattacharya puts it beautifully: "When Indian women say 'I am Draupadi,' they're not claiming victimhood; they're warning their oppressors that justice will eventually come, even if it requires burning everything to the ground." This reclaiming of Draupadi as a figure of righteous fury rather than sacrificial suffering marks a huge departure from traditional interpretations that emphasized her patience and devotion.

What's fascinating is how devotional practices have transformed Draupadi from primarily a literary character to a literal goddess. In parts of South India, especially Tamil Nadu, she's worshipped as Draupadi Amman, this fierce protective deity associated with fire. They have these annual fire-walking ceremonies that honor her power to protect devotees from harm. These practices aren't new - they're centuries old - but they've gained new significance as expressions of female power and agency. Anthropologist Don Handelman has documented how women who participate in these rituals explicitly connect them to their own experiences of overcoming violence and injustice.

Literary and artistic representations have further cemented Draupadi's status as a feminist icon. Chitra Banerjee Divakaruni's novel *The Palace of Illusions* (2008) retells the entire Mahabharata from Draupadi's perspective, portraying her as this complex figure whose strength comes not from supernatural power but from her intelligence, determination, and capacity to love despite betrayal. Divakaruni's Draupadi isn't some perfect heroine - she's a fully realized human being whose flaws (her pride, her vengeful anger, her destructive passion) are inseparable from her strengths.

Visual artists have similarly reclaimed Draupadi's image. The painter Arpana Caur's series depicts her not at the moment of divine rescue but in her rage afterward, with unbound hair and fierce expression, embodying the Sanskrit concept of *raudra rasa* (the aesthetic of fury). Performance artist Navjot Altaf's installations place Draupadi alongside contemporary women who have survived sexual violence, creating this transhistorical connection between mythic and modern experiences of female resilience.

These cultural reinterpretations have established Draupadi as what Wendy Doniger calls a "counter-model" to more passive female ideals in Hindu tradition. Unlike Sita from the Ramayana, who's often held up as this paragon of wifely devotion and patience, Draupadi refuses to accept injustice even when it comes from those she loves. Unlike Savitri, who saves her husband through unwavering devotion, Draupadi demands reciprocal loyalty and protection from her husbands and holds them accountable when they fail her. This counter-model gives contemporary Hindu women a religious framework for asserting their rights and dignity without having to reject their cultural heritage.

Modern Psychological and Sociological Analyses

The complexity of Draupadi's character and circumstances has made her catnip for modern psychological and sociological analysis. These approaches apply contemporary frameworks to understand both the character herself and the cultural significance of her unusual situation.

From a psychological perspective, several scholars have examined Draupadi through trauma theory. The multiple violations she experiences - being married against her will to five men, being staked in a gambling match, the attempted public disrobing, and twelve years of forest exile - constitute what we'd now call complex trauma. Her responses throughout the narrative, particularly her refusal to forgive or forget these violations, align with what trauma specialists recognize as healthy resistance to premature reconciliation. Psychologist Rashna Imhasly argues that Draupadi's unwavering demand for justice isn't vengefulness but the psychological necessity of acknowledgment and accountability for healing to happen.

The concept of resilience - adapting and thriving despite adversity - provides another lens for understanding Draupadi. Throughout the epic, she demonstrates remarkable psychological flexibility, adjusting to radically changed circumstances while maintaining her core values and sense of self. When exiled to the forest, she doesn't just survive - she creates a meaningful life for herself and her husbands. When serving incognito in King Virata's court, she strategically uses her skills and intelligence to secure protection while maintaining her dignity. These capacities reflect what positive psychology calls post-traumatic growth - deriving meaning and even strength from deeply challenging experiences.

Sociological analyses have focused on how Draupadi's polyandrous marriage reflects broader social structures. Anthropologist Leela Dube has compared the Pandava arrangement with ethnographic studies of polyandrous practices in certain Himalayan communities, where brothers commonly share a wife to prevent the division of limited agricultural land. This comparison suggests that the epic might preserve memory of actual social practices that existed in certain regions or periods of ancient India, despite being marginalized in later orthodox Hindu law codes.

Family systems theory provides another framework for understanding the complex dynamics of Draupadi's household. The multiple relationships create what sociologists would call a "high-boundary complexity" family system, with numerous opportunities for both alliance and conflict. Modern research on polyamorous families suggests that such arrangements require explicit negotiation of resources, attention, and power - precisely the issues that create dramatic tension throughout Draupadi's narrative. The epic's portrayal of these negotiations, though situated in an ancient context, resonates with contemporary studies of non-traditional family structures.

Gender performance theory, associated with scholars like Judith Butler, offers yet another lens. Throughout the epic, Draupadi must navigate contradictory expectations for female behavior: she must be sexually available to five husbands while maintaining standards of female purity; she must respect patriarchal authority while advocating for her own dignity; she must embody feminine gentleness while channeling righteous fury. These contradictions reveal the inherently performative nature of gender roles, as Draupadi constantly adapts her presentation of femininity to survive within oppressive structures while simultaneously challenging those structures.

Contemporary sociological analyses have also examined how Draupadi's story reflects intersecting systems of oppression. While gender forms the most obvious axis of her marginalization, her experiences are also shaped by caste politics (as evidenced in Karna's rejection of her at the svayamvara and Duryodhana's wife Bhanumati's caste-based insults) and by political status (as her treatment fluctuates dramatically based on whether her husbands hold power). This intersectional approach reveals Draupadi not simply as a woman navigating patriarchy but as a subject positioned within multiple overlapping systems of power and privilege.

What emerges from these modern psychological and sociological analyses is a remarkably contemporary understanding of Draupadi as a complex individual navigating multilayered social constraints. Far from being merely a literary character or religious archetype, she embodies psychological and social realities that remain relevant in today's world. Her negotiations of power, identity, trauma, and resilience speak directly to contemporary experiences, particularly for women managing multiple roles and relationships within still-patriarchal social structures.

Conclusion: Draupadi Beyond Traditional Frameworks

Contemporary feminist and modern interpretations have completely transformed how we understand Draupadi and her polyandrous marriage. By shifting focus from divine intervention or karmic explanation to questions of agency, power dynamics, symbolic significance, and psychological complexity, these approaches have revealed dimensions of the narrative that traditional interpretations often overlooked or minimized.

What emerges is a figure who transcends traditional categorizations of female characters in religious literature. Draupadi is neither an unambiguous victim nor a perfect heroine; neither a passive recipient of unusual circumstances nor entirely free from social constraints. Instead, she represents something more complex and ultimately more human: a woman navigating multilayered systems of power with intelligence, determination, occasional rage, and remarkable resilience.

The continuing fascination with Draupadi - evident in scholarly work, artistic representations, and personal devotion - suggests that her story speaks to something essential in the human experience, particularly for women. Her refusal to accept injustice, her demand that moral principles apply even to the powerful, and her insistence on maintaining her dignity despite humiliation resonate across cultural and historical boundaries. As we continue to engage with her story, Draupadi remains not just a character from an ancient epic but a living symbol of the ongoing struggle for justice, dignity, and agency in a world still shaped by unequal power relations.

CHAPTER FIVE

Folk Traditions, Art, and Performance: Draupadi Beyond the Text

Draupadi's story leaps off the written page and comes alive across countless folk traditions throughout South Asia. These local interpretations often take surprising turns away from the Sanskrit epic, showing how different communities have made sense of her controversial polyandrous marriage.

In Tamil Nadu, Draupadi isn't just a character - she's a full-fledged goddess. Known as Draupadiyamman, she's worshipped as a manifestation of divine feminine power. The annual Draupadi festivals there are intense affairs, with fire-walking rituals, spirit possession ceremonies, and dramatic performances that can last for nights on end. What's fascinating is how these folk traditions often celebrate her five marriages rather than apologizing for them. The villagers see her ability to maintain five husbands as proof of her extraordinary power - not as something that diminishes her virtue.

Travel to rural Rajasthan or Himachal Pradesh, and you'll hear ballads that offer more down-to-earth explanations for her unusual marriage. Some songs frame it as reflecting ancient tribal customs that once existed in these mountainous regions. These folk ballads tend to focus on Draupadi's impressive household management skills and her talent for keeping peace among the brothers. She's portrayed as the emotional glue that held the Pandava family together through all their struggles.

If you look at how artists have depicted Draupadi over the centuries, you can trace changing attitudes toward her marriages. Classical Pahari miniature paintings from the 18th century generally avoided showing her polyandrous situation directly - they'd typically show her with just one husband (usually Arjuna or Yudhishthira) in any given scene. But contemporary folk paintings, especially from eastern India, often boldly show Draupadi with all five husbands at once - suggesting a more open acknowledgment of this aspect of her story.

Perhaps the most vibrant window into how communities interpret Draupadi's marriage comes through performance traditions. The Yakshagana theater of Karnataka, the Kathakali of Kerala, and the Ramlila traditions of North India each present their own distinctive take. Kathakali performances often delve into Draupadi's emotional conflicts about her unusual marriage, while some Yakshagana adaptations emphasize divine sanction behind the arrangement. Most striking is the Draupadi Amman tradition in Tamil Nadu, where male performers become possessed by Draupadi, temporarily becoming vessels for her divine power.

Regional Variations: One Story, Many Interpretations

As the Mahabharata travels across regional and linguistic boundaries, Draupadi's polyandrous marriage undergoes fascinating transformations. These variations show how different communities have wrestled with the controversial aspects of her story, sometimes emphasizing divine explanations, sometimes practical considerations, and sometimes reimagining the narrative entirely.

The Bhil tribal version from central India, documented by anthropologist Verrier Elwin, presents her marriage as a practical arrangement reflecting actual Bhil customs of fraternal polyandry practiced in resource-poor environments. This interpretation downplays divine intervention in favor of social custom, framing the arrangement as logical rather than exceptional.

The Bengali tradition, especially as preserved in Kashiram Das's medieval Bengali Mahabharata, puts heavy emphasis on Draupadi's previous incarnation as a sage's daughter who prayed five separate times for a husband with different qualities. This strengthens the karmic justification, presenting the polyandrous marriage as fulfillment of divine justice rather than an oddity requiring explanation.

Kerala's Malayalam Mahabharata tradition, including the influential Bharatamala, develops a unique perspective by expanding Draupadi's role in the marriage decision. In some versions, she actively participates in the arrangement rather than merely accepting Kunti's mistaken instruction, suggesting her consent was meaningful rather than just acquiescent.

Most striking is the Draupadi cult of Tamil Nadu, where her worship often overshadows that of her husbands. In the Tamil tradition, Draupadi isn't just a human woman in an unusual marriage but a fiery goddess whose multiple husbands reflect her need for multiple consorts to channel her immense shakti (divine feminine energy). This theological reframing transforms what might be seen as a compromising situation into evidence of her supernatural status.

The Telugu Mahabharata tradition, particularly in Nannaya Bhatta's version, offers one of the most nuanced psychological explorations of the polyandrous marriage, dedicating significant text to Draupadi's private emotions and the complex dynamics between the brothers as they share a wife. This version humanizes the arrangement while maintaining its divine sanction.

These regional variations demonstrate how a single controversial narrative element can evolve to reflect local social customs, religious emphases, and cultural sensibilities. Hindu tradition hasn't enforced a uniform interpretation of Draupadi's story, but has allowed it to flourish in multiple, sometimes contradictory forms—each revealing different approaches to reconciling tradition with the complexities of human relationships.

Modern Literature and Media: Reimagining Draupadi

The last century has seen an explosion of creative reinterpretations of Draupadi's story across literature, film, television, and digital media. These modern adaptations often use her polyandrous marriage as a vehicle to explore contemporary issues of gender, autonomy, and religious tradition in rapidly changing societies.

Chitra Banerjee Divakaruni's novel "The Palace of Illusions" (2008) retells the Mahabharata from Draupadi's first-person perspective, giving readers an intimate psychological portrait of a woman navigating an arranged polyandrous marriage. Divakaruni's Draupadi struggles with the practical and emotional complications of loving five different men, favoring Arjuna while maintaining relationships with all her husbands. The novel breaks centuries of modest silence by directly depicting the sexual and romantic complexities of the arrangement.

Shashi Tharoor's satirical "The Great Indian Novel" (1989) transplants the Mahabharata onto India's independence movement and early political history, with Draupadi representing modern India herself. Her polyandrous marriage becomes a metaphor for the nation's complex relationship with competing political ideologies and foreign influences—a clever recontextualization that demonstrates the story's continuing metaphorical power.

Feminist writer Mahasweta Devi's Bengali short story "Draupadi" (1971) radically reimagines the character as a tribal revolutionary captured by government forces. Though not directly addressing the polyandrous marriage, the story reframes Draupadi's vulnerability and strength in a contemporary political context, showing how her character continues to serve as a powerful symbol of female resistance against patriarchal oppression.

The massively popular television serialization of the Mahabharata by B.R. Chopra (1988-1990) brought Draupadi's story into millions of households across India. This adaptation took a relatively conservative approach to depicting the polyandrous marriage, emphasizing its divine sanction and the brothers' strict arrangement for sharing time with their wife. Nevertheless, the series sparked widespread discussion about gender roles in Hindu tradition and introduced many viewers to aspects of Draupadi's story that simplified children's versions had omitted.

More recent productions, including the 2013-2014 television series directed by Siddharth Kumar Tewary, have attempted more psychologically nuanced portrayals of the polyandrous relationship, albeit still constrained by broadcast standards and popular sensibilities. The growing influence of feminist perspectives is evident in these newer adaptations, which tend to grant Draupadi greater agency and emotional complexity.

Digital media has opened entirely new avenues for engaging with Draupadi's story. Web comics, YouTube channels, and podcasts now offer interpretations that would never pass traditional gatekeepers of religious narrative. Platforms like "Epified" create animated videos explaining the philosophical dimensions of Draupadi's marriages, while feminist podcasts analyze the power dynamics of her relationships through contemporary theoretical frameworks.

These modern reinterpretations demonstrate how Draupadi's unusual marriage continues to provide fertile ground for exploring perennial questions about women's autonomy, divine will versus human choice, and the negotiation of desire within social constraints. Rather than fading into irrelevance, her story has gained new resonance in an era grappling with changing definitions of marriage, gender, and religious tradition.

Contemporary Hindu Practitioners: Reconciling Tradition and Modernity

For Hindus today, especially those navigating between traditional religious frameworks and modern social values, Draupadi's polyandrous marriage presents both challenges and opportunities. How individuals and communities reconcile this controversial element of sacred text reveals much about the adaptive strategies employed in living religious traditions.

Orthodox Hindu commentators often emphasize the exceptional nature of Draupadi's marriage, presenting it as a divinely sanctioned anomaly rather than a precedent. The influential Gita Press publications, for example, stress that the arrangement was unique to its specific mythological context and approved by sages and gods for special reasons that don't apply to ordinary humans. This approach preserves the sanctity of the text while maintaining modern brahmanical norms of female monogamy.

Progressive Hindu theologians, by contrast, often point to Draupadi's story as evidence that Hindu tradition contains within itself the seeds of more flexible gender arrangements than later orthodox interpretations would suggest. They argue that the presence of approved polyandry in a foundational text demonstrates Hinduism's inherent adaptability and plurality of acceptable family structures. Organizations like Arsha Vidya have published commentaries suggesting that the Mahabharata demonstrates how dharma (righteous duty) must sometimes be contextual rather than absolute.

For many ordinary Hindu practitioners, Draupadi's marriage becomes most comprehensible when viewed through a devotional rather than legal framework. When anthropologist Don Handelman spoke with devotees at Draupadi temples in Tamil Nadu, he found that worshippers often described her multiple marriages as evidence of her extraordinary capacity for love and devotion. Rather than seeing the arrangement as compromising her position, they viewed it as demonstration of her superhuman qualities.

Hindu feminist scholars and practitioners have developed particularly nuanced approaches to Draupadi's story. Scholars like Rita Gross and Vasudha Narayanan suggest that the presence of polyandry in the Mahabharata provides textual authority for questioning patriarchal marriage norms that developed in later periods. They argue that Hindu women can look to Draupadi as a model of a woman who maintained her dignity, agency, and spiritual power despite being embedded in complex patriarchal arrangements.

The diaspora Hindu experience adds another dimension to contemporary interpretations. For Hindus in North America, Europe, and elsewhere, explaining Draupadi's marriage to non-Hindu friends and colleagues can prompt deeper reflection on aspects of tradition often taken for granted. Community discussions in temples and cultural organizations frequently address how to present complex elements of Hindu epics to children growing up in societies with different values and assumptions about marriage and gender.

Perhaps most striking is how Draupadi's polyandrous marriage serves different rhetorical functions in different contexts. In discussions about Hindu tradition's historical flexibility, it may be cited as evidence of once-permitted alternatives to monogamy. In conversations about feminist reinterpretations of sacred texts, it can represent either female oppression or remarkable female power, depending on the interpreter's perspective. In interfaith dialogues, it might illustrate Hinduism's comfort with narrative complexity and moral ambiguity compared to more doctrinally rigid traditions.

What emerges from these diverse approaches is not a single authoritative interpretation of Draupadi's marriage but rather a demonstration of Hinduism's remarkable capacity for containing multiple, sometimes contradictory perspectives within a shared tradition. The controversy itself becomes productive—generating new theological insights, artistic expressions, and communal conversations that keep the tradition vibrant and relevant across changing social contexts.

For contemporary Hindu practitioners, Draupadi thus remains not merely a character from ancient text but a living presence whose complicated story continues to challenge, inspire, and occasionally disturb. Her polyandrous marriage—neither wholly embraced nor rejected by tradition—creates a space for ongoing negotiation between textual authority, lived experience, and evolving understandings of gender and relationship. In this tension lies much of her enduring power.

Conclusion: Draupadi's Legacy

Synthesis of Perspectives: Many Truths in One Story

Draupadi's story leaps off the written page and comes alive across countless folk traditions throughout South Asia. These local interpretations often take surprising turns away from the Sanskrit epic, showing how different communities have made sense of her controversial polyandrous marriage.

In Tamil Nadu, Draupadi isn't just a character - she's a full-fledged goddess. Known as Draupadiyamman, she's worshipped as a manifestation of divine feminine power. The annual Draupadi festivals there are intense affairs, with fire-walking rituals, spirit possession ceremonies, and dramatic performances that can last for nights on end. What's fascinating is how these folk traditions often celebrate her five marriages rather than apologizing for them. The villagers see her ability to maintain five husbands as proof of her extraordinary power - not as something that diminishes her virtue.

Travel to rural Rajasthan or Himachal Pradesh, and you'll hear ballads that offer more down-to-earth explanations for her unusual marriage. Some songs frame it as reflecting ancient tribal customs that once existed in these mountainous regions. These folk ballads tend to focus on Draupadi's impressive household management skills and her talent for keeping peace among the brothers. She's portrayed as the emotional glue that held the Pandava family together through all their struggles.

If you look at how artists have depicted Draupadi over the centuries, you can trace changing attitudes toward her marriages. Classical Pahari miniature paintings from the 18th century generally avoided showing her polyandrous situation directly - they'd typically show her with just one husband (usually Arjuna or Yudhishthira) in any given scene. But contemporary folk paintings, especially from eastern India, often boldly show Draupadi with all five husbands at once - suggesting a more open acknowledgment of this aspect of her story.

Perhaps the most vibrant window into how communities interpret Draupadi's marriage comes through performance traditions. The Yakshagana theater of Karnataka, the Kathakali of Kerala, and the Ramlila traditions of North India each present their own distinctive take. Kathakali performances often delve into Draupadi's emotional conflicts about her unusual marriage, while some Yakshagana adaptations emphasize divine sanction behind the arrangement. Most striking is the Draupadi Amman tradition in Tamil Nadu, where male performers become possessed by Draupadi, temporarily becoming vessels for her divine power.

Regional Variations: One Story, Many Interpretations

As the Mahabharata travels across regional and linguistic boundaries, Draupadi's polyandrous marriage undergoes fascinating transformations. These variations show how different communities have wrestled with the controversial aspects of her story, sometimes emphasizing divine explanations, sometimes practical considerations, and sometimes reimagining the narrative entirely.

The Bhil tribal version from central India, documented by anthropologist Verrier Elwin, presents her marriage as a practical arrangement reflecting actual Bhil customs of fraternal polyandry practiced in resource-poor environments. This interpretation downplays divine intervention in favor of social custom, framing the arrangement as logical rather than exceptional.

The Bengali tradition, especially as preserved in Kashiram Das's medieval Bengali Mahabharata, puts heavy emphasis on Draupadi's previous incarnation as a sage's daughter who prayed five separate times for a husband with different qualities. This strengthens the karmic justification, presenting the polyandrous marriage as fulfillment of divine justice rather than an oddity requiring explanation.

Kerala's Malayalam Mahabharata tradition, including the influential Bharatamala, develops a unique perspective by expanding Draupadi's role in the marriage decision. In some versions, she actively participates in the arrangement rather than merely accepting Kunti's mistaken instruction, suggesting her consent was meaningful rather than just acquiescent.

Most striking is the Draupadi cult of Tamil Nadu, where her worship often overshadows that of her husbands. In the Tamil tradition, Draupadi isn't just a human woman in an unusual marriage but a fiery goddess whose multiple husbands reflect her need for multiple consorts to channel her immense shakti (divine feminine energy). This theological reframing transforms what might be seen as a compromising situation into evidence of her supernatural status.

The Telugu Mahabharata tradition, particularly in Nannaya Bhatta's version, offers one of the most nuanced psychological explorations of the polyandrous marriage, dedicating significant text to Draupadi's private emotions and the complex dynamics between the brothers as they share a wife. This version humanizes the arrangement while maintaining its divine sanction.

These regional variations demonstrate how a single controversial narrative element can evolve to reflect local social customs, religious emphases, and cultural sensibilities. Hindu tradition hasn't enforced a uniform interpretation of Draupadi's story, but has allowed it to flourish in multiple, sometimes contradictory forms—each revealing different approaches to reconciling tradition with the complexities of human relationships.

Modern Literature and Media: Reimagining Draupadi

The last century has seen an explosion of creative reinterpretations of Draupadi's story across literature, film, television, and digital media. These modern adaptations often use her polyandrous marriage as a vehicle to explore contemporary issues of gender, autonomy, and religious tradition in rapidly changing societies.

Chitra Banerjee Divakaruni's novel "The Palace of Illusions" (2008) retells the Mahabharata from Draupadi's first-person perspective, giving readers an intimate psychological portrait of a woman navigating an arranged polyandrous marriage. Divakaruni's Draupadi struggles with the practical and emotional complications of loving five different men, favoring Arjuna while maintaining relationships with all her husbands. The novel breaks centuries of modest silence by directly depicting the sexual and romantic complexities of the arrangement.

Shashi Tharoor's satirical "The Great Indian Novel" (1989) transplants the Mahabharata onto India's independence movement and early political history, with Draupadi representing modern India herself. Her polyandrous marriage becomes a metaphor for the nation's complex relationship with competing political ideologies and foreign influences—a clever recontextualization that demonstrates the story's continuing metaphorical power.

Feminist writer Mahasweta Devi's Bengali short story "Draupadi" (1971) radically reimagines the character as a tribal revolutionary captured by government forces. Though not directly addressing the polyandrous marriage, the story reframes Draupadi's vulnerability and strength in a contemporary political context, showing how her character continues to serve as a powerful symbol of female resistance against patriarchal oppression.

The massively popular television serialization of the Mahabharata by B.R. Chopra (1988-1990) brought Draupadi's story into millions of households across India. This adaptation took a relatively conservative approach to depicting the polyandrous marriage, emphasizing its divine sanction and the brothers' strict arrangement for sharing time with their wife. Nevertheless, the series sparked widespread discussion about gender roles in Hindu tradition and introduced many viewers to aspects of Draupadi's story that simplified children's versions had omitted.

More recent productions, including the 2013-2014 television series directed by Siddharth Kumar Tewary, have attempted more psychologically nuanced portrayals of the polyandrous relationship, albeit still constrained by broadcast standards and popular sensibilities. The growing influence of feminist perspectives is evident in these newer adaptations, which tend to grant Draupadi greater agency and emotional complexity.

Digital media has opened entirely new avenues for engaging with Draupadi's story. Web comics, YouTube channels, and podcasts now offer interpretations that would never pass traditional gatekeepers of religious narrative. Platforms like "Epified" create animated videos explaining the philosophical dimensions of Draupadi's marriages, while feminist podcasts analyze the power dynamics of her relationships through contemporary theoretical frameworks.

These modern reinterpretations demonstrate how Draupadi's unusual marriage continues to provide fertile ground for exploring perennial questions about women's autonomy, divine will versus human choice, and the negotiation of desire within social constraints. Rather than fading into irrelevance, her story has gained new resonance in an era grappling with changing definitions of marriage, gender, and religious tradition.

Contemporary Hindu Practitioners: Reconciling Tradition and Modernity

For Hindus today, especially those navigating between traditional religious frameworks and modern social values, Draupadi's polyandrous marriage presents both challenges and opportunities. How individuals and communities reconcile this controversial element of sacred text reveals much about the adaptive strategies employed in living religious traditions.

Orthodox Hindu commentators often emphasize the exceptional nature of Draupadi's marriage, presenting it as a divinely sanctioned anomaly rather than a precedent. The influential Gita Press publications, for example, stress that the arrangement was unique to its specific mythological context and approved by sages and gods for special reasons that don't apply to ordinary humans. This approach preserves the sanctity of the text while maintaining modern brahmanical norms of female monogamy.

Progressive Hindu theologians, by contrast, often point to Draupadi's story as evidence that Hindu tradition contains within itself the seeds of more flexible gender arrangements than later orthodox interpretations would suggest. They argue that the presence of approved polyandry in a foundational text demonstrates Hinduism's inherent adaptability and plurality of acceptable family structures. Organizations like Arsha Vidya have published commentaries suggesting that the Mahabharata demonstrates how dharma (righteous duty) must sometimes be contextual rather than absolute.

For many ordinary Hindu practitioners, Draupadi's marriage becomes most comprehensible when viewed through a devotional rather than legal framework. When anthropologist Don Handelman spoke with devotees at Draupadi temples in Tamil Nadu, he found that worshippers often described her multiple marriages as evidence of her extraordinary capacity for love and devotion. Rather than seeing the arrangement as compromising her position, they viewed it as demonstration of her superhuman qualities.

Hindu feminist scholars and practitioners have developed particularly nuanced approaches to Draupadi's story. Scholars like Rita Gross and Vasudha Narayanan suggest that the presence of polyandry in the Mahabharata provides textual authority for questioning patriarchal marriage norms that developed in later periods. They argue that Hindu women can look to Draupadi as a model of a woman who maintained her dignity, agency, and spiritual power despite being embedded in complex patriarchal arrangements.

The diaspora Hindu experience adds another dimension to contemporary interpretations. For Hindus in North America, Europe, and elsewhere, explaining Draupadi's marriage to non-Hindu friends and colleagues can prompt deeper reflection on aspects of tradition often taken for granted. Community discussions in temples and cultural organizations frequently address how to present complex elements of Hindu epics to children growing up in societies with different values and assumptions about marriage and gender.

Perhaps most striking is how Draupadi's polyandrous marriage serves different rhetorical functions in different contexts. In discussions about Hindu tradition's historical flexibility, it may be cited as evidence of once-permitted alternatives to monogamy. In conversations about feminist reinterpretations of sacred texts, it can represent either female oppression or remarkable female power, depending on the interpreter's perspective. In interfaith dialogues, it might illustrate Hinduism's comfort with narrative complexity and moral ambiguity compared to more doctrinally rigid traditions.

What emerges from these diverse approaches is not a single authoritative interpretation of Draupadi's marriage but rather a demonstration of Hinduism's remarkable capacity for containing multiple, sometimes contradictory perspectives within a shared tradition. The controversy itself becomes productive—generating new theological insights, artistic expressions, and communal conversations that keep the tradition vibrant and relevant across changing social contexts.

For contemporary Hindu practitioners, Draupadi thus remains not merely a character from ancient text but a living presence whose complicated story continues to challenge, inspire, and occasionally disturb. Her polyandrous marriage—neither wholly embraced nor rejected by tradition—creates a space for ongoing negotiation between textual authority, lived experience, and evolving understandings of gender and relationship. In this tension lies much of her enduring power.

Conclusion: Draupadi's Legacy

Synthesis of Perspectives: Many Truths in One Story

The story of Draupadi's polyandrous marriage reveals something remarkable about both the Mahabharata and Hindu tradition itself - its capacity to hold multiple truths simultaneously. From ancient commentators seeking divine justification to feminist scholars interpreting it as a subversion of patriarchy, each reading offers a valid lens through which to understand this complex arrangement.

Religious perspectives focus on cosmic purpose - Draupadi as the goddess Shri incarnate, fulfilling a divine plan beyond ordinary moral boundaries. Her marriage becomes not a model to follow but an exceptional arrangement with mystical significance, her five husbands representing different aspects of divinity.

Historical analyses point to more practical origins. Evidence of fraternal polyandry among certain ancient Indo-Aryan groups suggests the narrative might reflect actual social practices from times when resource scarcity and inheritance concerns led some communities to develop alternative family structures. The later shift toward strict female monogamy in Hindu texts could show the gradual dominance of certain religious frameworks over others.

Feminist readings center on questions of agency and power. Was Draupadi empowered or objectified? The text itself is ambiguous - she demonstrates remarkable independence in many episodes yet appears constrained by her unusual marital position in others. This very ambiguity has allowed her to become a powerful symbol in contemporary discussions about women's autonomy.

What emerges isn't a single theory but an acknowledgment that mythological narratives work on multiple levels simultaneously. Draupadi's marriage functions as cosmic metaphor, historical reflection, psychological exploration, and social commentary all at once. The story's enduring power lies precisely in this richness - its ability to generate meaning across different interpretive frameworks rather than collapsing into a single explanation.

The Enduring Relevance: Draupadi in Contemporary Consciousness

Despite being rooted in an ancient text, Draupadi's story shows remarkable resilience in today's culture. Far from fading into obscurity as a troublesome anomaly, her narrative continues to inspire, provoke, and challenge modern audiences in multiple domains.

In literature, Draupadi has become central to reimagining classical narratives from female perspectives. Works like Divakaruni's "The Palace of Illusions" and Ray's "Yajnaseni" place her consciousness at the epic's center, inviting readers to experience the Mahabharata through her eyes. These retellings explore her polyandrous marriage as both trauma and potential empowerment, delving into the inner life of a woman navigating extraordinary circumstances.

In political discourse, she serves as a powerful symbol of feminine resistance to humiliation and injustice. Her moment in the royal court—questioning the foundations of a social order that would allow her to be gambled away—resonates with contemporary movements against gender-based violence. Her marriage itself becomes a metaphor for women burdened by multiple, sometimes conflicting social expectations.

In religious practice, devotional traditions surrounding Draupadi (particularly in South India where she is sometimes worshipped as a goddess) show how controversial elements of scripture can be transformed through devotional frameworks. Rather than being eliminated from religious consciousness, her complex story has been incorporated into lived traditions celebrating her as an embodiment of female power and divine justice.

In popular media, televised adaptations of the Mahabharata have brought Draupadi into millions of homes. These productions must negotiate the tension between traditional interpretations and contemporary sensibilities, particularly regarding her marriage. How they portray the polyandrous arrangement reflects evolving attitudes toward gender and marriage in modern Hindu society.

This continued engagement suggests that controversial narratives often prove most generative for cultural reflection. Rather than being marginalized, her polyandrous marriage has become a crucial site for ongoing negotiation of Hindu identity, gender roles, and ethical frameworks.

The Flexibility of Tradition: What Draupadi Reveals About Hinduism

Draupadi's polyandrous marriage offers a powerful case study in the inherent flexibility of Hindu tradition. Despite later dharmashastra texts explicitly condemning polyandry, this arrangement—prominently featured in one of Hinduism's most sacred narratives—has never been excised. Instead, it has been interpreted, contextualized, and sometimes problematized, but always retained as an integral part of the sacred narrative.

This persistence reveals several important characteristics of Hindu tradition:

First, it demonstrates that Hindu scripture prioritizes narrative integrity over doctrinal consistency. Unlike traditions that might edit or remove problematic elements to maintain theological coherence, Hindu texts preserve contradictions and complexities, trusting practitioners to navigate these tensions through interpretation rather than elimination.

Second, it illustrates how Hindu tradition has historically accommodated multiple, sometimes contradictory practices through contextualization rather than universal pronouncement. The same tradition that preserves stories of Draupadi's polyandry also produced texts condemning the practice. Rather than resolving this contradiction, Hindu thought typically deploys concepts of yuga (cosmic age), adhikara (spiritual qualification), and apaddharma (emergency ethics) to explain how practices appropriate in one context might be inappropriate in another.

Third, it highlights the distinction between exemplary and exceptional narratives. Hindu texts contain numerous episodes understood as exceptional circumstances not meant for general emulation. Draupadi's marriage falls into this category—divinely sanctioned for specific cosmic purposes but not established as a model for ordinary families.

Finally, Draupadi's story reveals how lived Hinduism often diverges from textual orthodoxy. While scholarly traditions might struggle to reconcile her polyandrous marriage with later dharmic injunctions, popular devotion to Draupadi has continued unabated, particularly in regional traditions less concerned with textual reconciliation than with the immediate power of her narrative.

This flexibility isn't relativism or lack of ethical framework. Rather, it reflects a tradition that has consistently valued contextual application of principles over rigid uniformity, and narrative wisdom over systematic theology.

Final Reflections: The Persistent Power of Controversial Narratives

Why do controversial narrative elements like Draupadi's marriage persist and remain meaningful across vast stretches of time and cultural change? What gives this particular story such enduring power?

Perhaps the answer lies in the nature of controversy itself. Stories that trouble us, that resist easy categorization or moral resolution, demand ongoing engagement. They cannot be simply absorbed and forgotten but must be continually reinterpreted as cultural contexts evolve. The very aspects of Draupadi's story that have made it controversial—its challenge to gender norms, its complex moral implications, its extraordinary circumstances—are precisely what have kept it alive in cultural consciousness.

Moreover, controversial narratives often touch upon fundamental tensions within human experience that transcend particular historical moments. Draupadi's story engages perennial questions: the relationship between divine decree and human choice, the tension between individual desire and social obligation, the balance of power between genders, the limits of devotion and sacrifice. These questions remain as relevant today as they were when the Mahabharata took its current form.

Draupadi herself embodies contradiction—divine yet human, powerful yet vulnerable, central to the narrative yet often objectified within it. Her polyandrous marriage magnifies these contradictions, placing her in a position simultaneously exceptional and constrained. This complexity makes her not a simple role model or cautionary tale, but something far more valuable: a figure through whom we can examine the constraints and possibilities of human lives shaped by forces both within and beyond our control.

In an age of increasing polarization, when complex narratives are often reduced to simplistic moral pronouncements, Draupadi's story offers a different model of engagement with difficult subject matter. It invites us not to resolve contradiction through dogmatic assertion, but to dwell within complexity, allowing multiple interpretations to coexist and illuminate one another.

The persistence of Draupadi's controversial marriage across three millennia suggests that religious and cultural traditions remain vital not by eliminating their problematic elements, but by continually reengaging them. Each generation faces anew the challenge of interpreting her extraordinary life, finding within it reflections of their own questions, struggles, and aspirations. In this ongoing conversation between ancient text and contemporary consciousness, Draupadi continues to emerge not as a distant figure from mythology, but as a living presence whose story remains unfinished—still generating meaning, still provoking thought, still inspiring devotion and debate in equal measure.

Shampa Chatterjee

Shampa Chatterjee is an Mindset and Relationship Coach, and the author of *The Art of Relationship Resonance-Mastering Communication For Stronger Bonds*. She is the founder of **Mind Wave Hub powered by Trustworthy Ties** and the visionary to empowers individuals and couples to enhance their relationships and overall mental well-being through mindset, mindfulness, movement, and meaningful conversations.

With a deep-rooted passion for **mythology**, Shampa reimagines sacred stories through a therapeutic and feminine lens—honoring the emotional endurance, quiet strength, and forgotten voices of women from epic narratives. Her work creates a powerful bridge between the **ancient and the modern**, the **spiritual and the psychological**.

She is the author of the acclaimed book *The Art Of Relationship Resonance: Mastering Communication For Stronger Bonds*—a transformative guide for building deeper, authentic connections. Her current book, part of the *Vows & Voids* series, continues this journey of emotional exploration, focusing on the often-unheard voices of women who waited, endured, and healed.

Shampa believes healing isn't linear — it's a courageous act of returning to ourselves again and again. Through her courses, coaching, events, and books, she continues to guide thousands toward greater awareness, mental and emotional wellness, and empowered living.

Through books, immersive retreats, digital courses, and mindful cycling journeys, Shampa empowers women to rise from relationship challenges with grace, clarity, and inner power.

When she's not mentoring soulpreneurs or retelling mythology under moonlight, you'll find her cycling through nature and mountains, journaling by candlelight, or sipping warm coffee while dreaming of her next retreat.

To connect with Shampa or learn more about her programs, visit:

- ? learn.trustworthyties.com
- ? connect@trustworthyties.com
- ? Instagram: @shampachatterjee

- ? Facebook: Shampa Chatterjee
- ?? Podcast: *Trustworthy Ties Show: The Soulful Relationship Series* (coming soon)

About The Author

Shampa Chatterjee

Shampa Chatterjee is an Mindset and Relationship Coach, and the author of *The Art of Relationship Resonance-Mastering Communication For Stronger Bonds.* She is the founder of **Mind Wave Hub powered by Trustworthy Ties** and the visionary to empowers individuals and couples to enhance their relationships and overall mental well-being through mindset, mindfulness, movement, and meaningful conversations.

With a deep-rooted passion for **mythology**, Shampa reimagines sacred stories through a therapeutic and feminine lens—honoring the emotional endurance, quiet strength, and forgotten voices of women from epic narratives. Her work creates a powerful bridge between the **ancient and the modern**, the **spiritual and the psychological**.

She is the author of the acclaimed book *The Art Of Relationship Resonance: Mastering Communication For Stronger Bonds*—a transformative guide for building deeper, authentic connections. Her current book, part of the *Vows & Voids* series, continues this journey of emotional exploration, focusing on the often-unheard voices of women who waited, endured, and healed.

Shampa believes healing isn't linear — it's a courageous act of returning to ourselves again and again. Through her courses, coaching, events, and books, she continues to guide thousands toward greater awareness, mental and emotional wellness, and empowered living.

Through books, immersive retreats, digital courses, and mindful cycling journeys, Shampa empowers women to rise from relationship challenges with grace, clarity, and inner power.

When she's not mentoring soulpreneurs or retelling mythology under moonlight, you'll find her cycling through nature and mountains, journaling by candlelight, or sipping warm coffee while dreaming of her next retreat.

To connect with Shampa or learn more about her programs, visit:

- ? learn.trustworthyties.com
- ? connect@trustworthyties.com
- ? Instagram: @shampachatterjee

- ? Facebook: Shampa Chatterjee
- ?? Podcast: *Trustworthy Ties Show: The Soulful Relationship Series* (coming soon)

Draupadi's Choice: Examining Polyandry In Hindu Mythology